To Marion

Cornelia

by

Jane J

best wishes

Jane Jones-

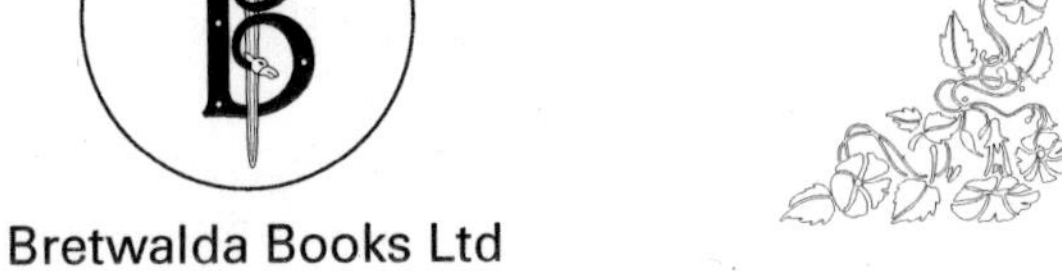

Bretwalda Books Ltd

First Published 2012

Bretwalda Books
Unit 8, Fir Tree Close, Epsom, Surrey KT17 3LD
www.BretwaldaBooks.com

To receive an e-catalogue of our complete range of books
send an email to info@BretwaldaBooks.com

ISBN 978-1-907791-39-0

Bretwalda Books Ltd

Chapter One

Cornelia lay back in the new hay up in the hayloft and chewed dreamily on a grassy stalk. Her knees were comfortably bent and her right leg was crossed over left. Her right sandal was hanging loosely from the end of her toe, which she was slowly bouncing up and down in the shimmering beam of dust motes that hung in the sunlight slanting through the open window hatch. Hector, her pet dog, lay below on the floor of the barn.

The voice of Paulus drifted clearly to her from across the yard.

"Will this be enough?" he asked as he heaved a large bundle of faggots off his back and dumped them on the ground near the opening of the hypocaust. From the open side of the barn Cornelia could see the bathhouse at the other side of the yard. She saw Paulus and noticed how his muscles shone with sweat as he twisted to unload his burden, but could not see the person to whom his question was addressed. Suddenly a flurry of mouldering leaves and rubbish came out of the fire hole of the hypocaust followed by the rear end of Nicomedes. His working tunic rose above his nether regions as he crawled backwards exposing his skinny bare backside. Cornelia giggled quietly to herself.

"That should do for kindling," he said,"now hitch up the ass and bring over a cartload of charcoal from the store."

"Oh good," thought Cornelia,"by tomorrow the bath water should be hot."

During the hot summer months she did not miss the bath. Up stream from where the cattle drank her father had had the slaves dig out a large basin where it was possible to swim and bathe in the cool waters.

The bath was very different. The walls of these rooms were also heated and were smoothly plastered and bore frescoes of delicate flora and fauna with elegant figures of people her mother told her were Greek gods and goddesses. The front of the house faced the road but at the back a garden sloped down towards the brook. In the garden were a number of fruit trees and beyond these were various workshops and slaves quarters. Nicomedes lived there in a small house with his son, Paulus. Nicomedes was born into Cornelia's family but his own father had been brought to Britain by a Roman soldier who had acquired him as part of his booty after a battle in some far off land. The soldier had fallen on impecunious times due to gambling and had sold his slave to Cornelia's grandfather.

Suddenly Cornelia heard her name being called from the house. It was Amalia, her old nurse, calling her in for supper. To Cornelia Amalia seemed very old. She had been the nurse of Cornelia's mother and had come with her when she married. In fact she was barely fifty but to Cornelia's fifteen years this seemed positively ancient. Cornelia was very comfortable in her little pile of hay and was not going to move, but her young appetite got the better of her and she decided to go in and see what was for supper. She scrambled down the ladder and lazily crossed to the house.

"There you are," said Amalia, "I've been looking for you everywhere. My, what a state you're in. Go and wash your hands and face and comb your hair. Hurry, your mother is waiting."

Cornelia went to her bedroom where a slave poured water into a basin for her to wash then combed her hair for her. Her curls were of a rich dark auburn shade, the colour one could see in the heart of a cornelian and her mother had named her for this reason. This hair colour was not very common and it always drew admiring looks. Her mother told her that her grandmother had had such hair. She winced as the little slave girl snagged the tortoiseshell comb in the tangles.

"Ow!" she said, "be careful."

"Sorry my lady," she said. When her task was accomplished she tied a ribbon round Cornelia's head to keep the unruly curls off her face.

Her brief toilet completed Cornelia went through to the triclinium where her parents were already waiting. She took her place and a slave placed a plate of food before her. It was tender pieces of lamb in a spicy sauce with pine nuts and little white carrots floating in it. She attacked the dish eagerly and drank the goblet of wine and water that was poured for her.

"Cornelia, do you have to gobble your food so fast?" said her mother, Verina.

"Sorry, mother, but it tastes so good."

"It will taste even better if you eat it slowly."

"Where's Jo?" Cornelia asked.

Jo was her brother, Jovianus. He was seven years her senior and as such they had grown up almost separately. Cornelia knew that there had been other pregnancies between them but in most cases they had come to nothing, except for the second child that was born eleven months after Jovianus but had died within days. After Cornelia there had been a couple of pregnancies, which ended in the same unsatisfactory way as the others and since then there had been no more.

"He's gone to the military camp at Onna to see one of the commanders. They want a permanent contract for hay and they also want to buy vegetables and fruit as well as eggs," said her father, Gaius. "We should do quite well. I think we might have to buy a couple more slaves."

Gaius had inherited the farm and land from his father. By marrying Verina, the only daughter of a landowner on the other side of the downs, he had acquired a sizeable area of land as her dowry and the family had become very wealthy and very well established. Gaius had become a Roman citizen, which gave added status to all his family.

The dishes for the first course had been cleared away and the slaves were bringing in a selection of pies when Jovianus came into the room and after giving his parents the required greeting and gently pulling his sister's hair he flung himself down on the low couch and said,

"I'm exhausted, thirsty and famished," and he signalled to a slave to pour him a goblet of wine and water. He drank the wine in one go and motioned the slave to refill the goblet.

"How did things go?" asked his father.

"Very well. They"re sending over tomorrow to collect the first load of hay and some soldiers are going to come over from time to time to help gather the vegetables. Our men will be able to direct them so we shouldn't need any more slaves at present."

"You stink," said Cornelia. "Couldn't you wash yourself before coming to eat? You put me right off my food."

Her brother laughed.

"I've never known anything put you off your food before, little miss piggy."

"Don't call me names."

"That will do," said their mother. "As soon as you've had something to eat you will go and wash and change."

"This evening," said Gaius, "you must come into the library and you will explain to me what prices and terms have been agreed."

"And you, Cornelia, will sit with me and read your Greek to me," said Verina.

After dinner Cornelia joined her mother in the sitting room. The doors to the garden were open and the late afternoon sun was still bright. Verina sat in a cane armchair and took up a piece of cherry coloured woollen fabric that she was fashioning into a new robe for the winter. Cornelia sat on a low stool and unrolled her book. She had been taught to read both in Greek and her own Latin by Verina. Verina's family had had a Greek slave who taught her brothers. As the only girl she had been allowed to join their lessons and had proved herself to be a capable student and indeed enjoyed the deeply academic debates that had gone on in the schoolroom. Although after her marriage at the age of sixteen she had applied herself to the duties of a wife and mother she had never lost her love of learning and passed on as much as she could to Cornelia.

Cornelia was more of a tomboy than her mother had been but nonetheless had a very alert and inquiring mind, and though she only gave a very moderate account of herself where mathematics was concerned she loved stories, especially tales full of adventure and romance.

"Why did Aeneas leave Dido? He said he loved her."

"Because it was his duty to obey the gods. He was told to sail away to a new land and there he founded the city of Rome."

"Well why didn't Dido go with him? She loved him."

"One cannot always do what one's heart wishes. One has to obey the rules and do one's duty."

"Did you want to marry father?"

"Not at first, I was very nervous. But I grew to love him, and he has always been a very good husband."

"Well I shan't marry someone I don't want to, no matter what father says. In fact I probably shan't marry at all. I want to do lots of things."

"What sort of things?"

"I want to see different places. Don't think I don't love you all and that I don't like my home," she added hurriedly, "I do, but there are so many more interesting places. I want to see Rome."

Her mother looked pensive.

"That might be somewhat difficult. It's a very long journey and not at all possible for a young girl to make. How do you plan to set about it?"

Verina knew that contradicting her headstrong daughter would probably result in a fit of sulks. She had learned how best to handle Cornelia over the years and by dint of secret diplomacy she usually made her behave as desired.

"I don't know," said Cornelia, "I've only just thought about it."

"You might get to Rome one day if you married someone who took you there."

"Yes, well then I might get married, but I want to choose."

"Have you got anyone in mind?" asked her mother with a little smile.

"No, not at all. When I was little I thought I"d marry Paulus but of course now I'm grown up I realise I can't marry a slave."

"Who's marrying a slave?" asked her brother as he came into the room.

"No-one," said Cornelia, "don't pick up tail ends".

Jovianus sat down on a cane chair next to his mother. He was tall with dark smooth hair and deep brown eyes. His complexion was brown from days spent in the open air supervising the work of the estate. He had washed and changed as his mother had told him to and his clean white robe accentuated his tanned skin. Gaius entered the room and sat down on the couch.

"It's getting dark in here, how about some lights?"

"Cornelia, go and ask for lamps to be lit."

Cornelia did as she was bid and was followed back into the room by two slaves carrying lamps. They placed the lamps one on the cupboard against the wall and the other on an iron tripod near Verina's chair. One of the girls lit a taper from one of the lamps and used it to light another lamp that hung from a beam in the ceiling by three chains. The other slave closed the doors to the garden. All this was accomplished smoothly and silently and the two girls left the room.

"Will you play a game with me?" asked Cornelia of her brother.

"All right, just one, providing you don't cheat."

"I never cheat," she said indignantly, "I can't help it if I always win."

She set up the gaming board and coloured stones on a low table and the next hour passed in a noisy game, which Cornelia won, amidst much laughing and rivalry.

Later that night Gaius and Verina lay side by side in their bed.

"I think it's time we thought about what we should do with Cornelia," said Verina

"What do you mean?" said Gaius.

"I think she's beginning to get very restless."

"Do you think it's time to start looking for a husband for her?"

"I don't think so, not just yet. For a different girl I would say yes but I think if we presented Cordelia with a prospective husband she would rebel. She's not ready to settle into marriage and motherhood."

"Then what?"

"How about taking her to Londinium?"

"What!"

"Why not? None of us has ever actually been there and you can safely leave the running of things to Jovianus for a few weeks. We could go and get back before the weather turns, we could probably get back in time for the end of the harvest."

"Hmmm, I'll think about it," said Gaius, and turning on his side he fell asleep. Verina smiled gently into the darkness, knowing that her suggestion would bear fruit and that they would travel to the southern capital.

Next morning Cornelia was coming out of the triclinium when she heard the wheels of a cart on the road. She went to the main entrance to see who the visitor might be and on opening the door she came face to face with the most handsome young man she had ever seen. He was dressed in a short working tunic of a russet colour with a shiny brown leather belt around his waist and brown leather sandals that laced around his ankles. She recognised him for a soldier. He smiled at the sight of her and his smile displayed a set of white even teeth. Cornelia's heart seemed to be beating erratically.

"Could you tell your master we've come for the hay?" he said, indicating the cart in the roadway. The horse was well groomed and the harness was as shiny as the young man"s belt. Another soldier was sitting on the cart holding the reins and looking speculatively at Cornelia. At the young man's words Cornelia realised that he had taken her for a slave. She was about to stand on her dignity and berate him soundly for his error when she changed her mind.

"Carry on past the corner of the house and turn through the gate into the yard; and don't forget to shut the gate."

The soldier gave her a salute and another disarming smile and as he walked back to the cart he said,

"Thank you, my beautiful maid; I hope we will meet again."

Cornelia shut the door and went in search of Jovianus. He was at the other end of the garden outside the workshops talking to Nicomedes.

"The men are here for the hay," she said.

Jovianus made his way to the yard at the side of the house and Cornelia walked back up through the orchard. She decided to go to the barn. If she climbed up the ladder she would be able to watch them loading the hay from the floor below. On the way she plucked a rosy apple and once she was safely ensconced in her usual eyrie she sank her teeth into it.

Jovianus instructed the soldier to back the cart up to the open end of the barn then he called Paulus to come and help with the loading. He greeted the soldier who had come to the door and Cornelia, by the polite manner that her brother used, decided that this soldier must be of higher rank than his companion. The cart driver stood on the cart with a pitchfork whilst the other three, similarly armed, tossed forkfuls of hay up to him. Cornelia watched the activity with interest. Soon all four young men were sweating and their bodies were gleaming as their muscles rippled. She gazed at the limbs of the young soldier who was in charge and once more her heart did the funny little jig that it had done before. The cart was soon piled high and the soldiers were taking their leave. Cornelia did not want this beautiful young man to disappear and without thinking she did a strange thing. She shied her apple core at Jovianus. It hit him on the shoulder and he looked up in mid sentence to see where it had come from. He spotted Cornelia's auburn curls and impish smile peeping from the top of the ladder.

"Cornelia! What in Hades are you doing? Come down here and apologise."

Cornelia scrambled down the ladder and straightening her dress she sauntered towards her brother.

"What was that for?" he said.

"Sorry, I thought I"d toss my apple core to the horse, but you got in the way."

Jovianus obviously did not believe her but did not pursue the matter.

"Please excuse my little sister," he said, "we despair of her ever growing up."

"Your sister!" said the soldier, and Cornelia delighted in his evident discomfort. "I offer my apologies, I did not realise when I addressed you earlier. I hope you did not find me presumptuous."

"Not at all," said Cornelia.

Jovianus, not being privy to what had gone on before looked a little puzzled at the exchange but his breeding carried him through.

"Cornelia, this is Marcus. He is in charge of the supplies up at the camp."

"Good day, Marcus. I hope we will see you again."

"No doubt," said Marcus and gave one of his heart-stopping smiles.

"Perhaps we should offer some refreshment before they go back," said Cornelia to her brother.

"No thank you my lady," said Marcus quickly, "we have a great deal to do before the day is over. Perhaps just a drink of water."

"Certainly," said Jovianus. "Paulus," he said, "draw a bucket of water for these men, and one for the horse."

Paulus went to the old well that served the yard and did as he was bid without a word. Although his actions were perfectly polite Cornelia sensed a certain resentment as he handed a ladle of water from the bucket to Marcus. In fact Paulus had watched the exchange between Marcus and Cornelia from the sidelines, unnoticed by Cornelia. But he had noticed that she had eyes only for Marcus and he also noticed the way in which they both looked at each other. For the first time in his life he felt inferior and resented his status.

The cart drove out of the yard and Paulus shut the gate a little more forcefully than was necessary. Jovianus turned on his heel and walked back to the workshops and Paulus banged the bucket down next to the well. Cornelia looked at him and for the first time saw the thunder behind his eyes.

"What's up?" she asked.

"Nothing, my lady."

Paulus had never addressed her as "my lady" before. Cornelia was puzzled. As small children she and Paulus had been playmates and had never had a serious quarrel. They had often disagreed about their games but usually Cornelia got her own way. This cold attitude was new to her.

"Don't you think Marcus is handsome?" she said.

For some reason this was obviously the wrong thing to say because with the thunder still behind his eyes Paulus said

"Handsome is as handsome does."

"What do you mean?" asked Cornelia.

"It's easy to be handsome when you are free and earn money. Your brother is handsome, even your father is handsome in his way."

Suddenly she realised that Paulus was jealous. She still did not realise that his jealousy rose out of his feelings for herself, she thought his resentment came from his lowly status.

"Paulus, I think you are handsome."

She was always quick with a word or phrase to console someone or bring sunshine back into a cloudy situation. It did not occur to her that in this particular instance this was not the best thing to say. Paulus looked at her hopefully and the thunder faded from behind his eyes as he said

"Do you honestly?"

"Of course I do," she replied.

At that moment the situation was saved by the voice of

Nicomedes calling from the other side of the orchard. Paulus went to join him and Cornelia walked towards the house.

That evening after their meal Verina and Cornelia were sitting in their customary places before the open doors to the loggia. Verina put down her needlework and said

"How would you like to go to Londinium?"

For once Cornelia was speechless. Verina laughed.

"Well, don't you think you would like to go?"

"I"d love to go," said Cornelia excitedly. "When will we go? How long will we stay? Where shall we sleep?"

"One thing at a time. We will go soon because your father wants to be back in time for the end of the harvest, so we will stay about seven days or so. We'll stay in an inn."

"Who's coming? Will Jo come?"

"No, as father will be away Jo will have to stay here and look after things. We'll probably take Paulus."

"I must go and look through my clothes and see what I shall wear. I'm glad the weather's warm, we won't need thick things."

So saying she hurried from the room and went to inspect the contents of the chest in her room. Tunics and cloaks were pulled out and flew about. Jewellery was taken from its small box and laid out to view. Her maid came to see what was to do.

"Florens, I'm going to Londinium," said Cornelia. "I shall need lots of clean clothes. What shall I take?"

"The pale green is nice, lady; it suits you very well. What about the russet cloak? It might not be warm all the time."

"You're right," she replied, and the next half hour was spent in a deep discussion about the merits of various outfits. Cornelia was sure that she would never get to sleep that night but by the time darkness fell she was fast asleep and dreaming of all she would see in Londinium.

Chapter Two

Two days later the sturdiest pony was hitched to the market cart which Paulus and his father had loaded the night before with boxes of apples, half a dozen round, yellow cheeses and a barrel of salted pork which Gaius wanted to sell in the city. He could get better prices there for his produce than he could locally. Gaius and Paulus sat on the seat behind the pony, Paulus holding the reins. Cornelia and her mother were very comfortably installed in the cart sitting on their rolled up bed linen and blankets. At her feet Verina had a basket of provisions for the journey.

The sun was barely up when Paulus shook the reins and gave a command to the pony and the little equipage wheeled out of the yard gate onto the road. Hector was barking furiously and straining to follow but Jovianus had him firmly by the collar. He had never been separated from his adored mistress in all his short life and wanted desperately to follow her.

"Shut him in my room till we're gone," Cornelia shouted.

Hector had been the smallest of a fine litter that their best bitch had produced. The day after they had been born Cornelia had gone to see them. There were five sturdy little puppies climbing over one another in search of food. Cornelia had leaned on the wooden beam that separated the corner stall where Bella lay and watched as they each found a nipple and settled down to suckle, except one who was nosing blindly in the wrong spot and being kicked away by one of his brothers.

Cornelia had crawled under the bar and taking the little runt gently in her hand she had put his little pink mouth to the remaining teat and watched with pleasure as he started to suckle. Jovianus had come into the barn at that point and had seen her on her knees in the straw. He had come over and leaning on the beam he had smiled at the scene.

"Not a bad litter," he had said. "They should fetch a good price, except for that little one. I think we'll drown him, the last one seldom does any good."

Cornelia had been horrified at his words.

"You can't drown him, he's sweet."

"But he'll never come to anything," her brother had declared.

"Yes he will, and anyway, I don't care, I want him."

"Very well, little sister, you have him."

So he had become Cornelia's own puppy. She had seen him as brave and sturdy and so she named him Hector. She had visited the little family every day and made sure that Hector got his fair share. She had been the first person he had seen when his eyes opened and she had been the one that rescued him when he had been bullied by his brothers. Once they were weaned Cornelia had brought him into the house and trained him not to foul the floors. He had slept under her bed and followed her everywhere. He slowly grew into a very handsome dog, though a little small for his breed. He was brown from the tips of his ears to the end of his tail. His eyes were brown and even his damp nose was brown. His coat shone like a new horse chestnut when it breaks out of its spiky green covering for the first time.

The travelling party made good progress because the road was in good condition and in no time at all they were on the metalled road that led to Londinium. The sun was high in the sky when they were passing over high country. The vistas all around were beautiful. The huge dome of the late summer sky was blue and cloudless and high above them birds were wheeling and dipping. The countryside around was green and wooded with here and there open fields in which the wheat was almost ready for the scythe. In the distance a plume of smoke from some farm kitchen rose straight up and disappeared in the heavens.

Towards midday they all descended from the cart and

Paulus gave the pony some food. Cornelia and her mother went into the bushes at the roadside to answer the call of nature then Verina unpacked the basket of provisions and set the food out on the tail of the cart. She handed each person a flat cake of bread, a piece of rich cheese and some slices from a large, crisp onion. Paulus sat apart from them and ate his food silently. Gaius took a leather bottle from the cart and some beakers and poured wine and water. After their frugal repast Gaius said

"Let's get on our way; I want to get more than half way before nightfall."

Verina packed up the food again and with Gaius" help climbed back into the cart.

"I"d like to walk for a while father, I get so stiff just sitting."

"Very well, I'll take the reins. Paulus you stretch your legs and walk for a few miles."

Cornelia reached into the cart and took two apples. She handed one to Paulus and bit into the other. The two young people walked side by side behind the cart chatting happily about their surroundings and commenting on the variations of flora. The road started to slope downwards and Paulus went to the front and held the horse's bridle to prevent him from going too fast down the hill. At the bottom of the hill the road went over a bridge that crossed a stream. Gaius halted the cart and Paulus, taking a pail from under the driving board scrambled down the bank and filled the pail for the horse. The pony drank long and deep then lifting his muzzle he snorted and sprayed Paulus with water. They all laughed as Paulus stowed the bucket back under the seat. Gaius flicked the reins and ordered the horse to continue. Paulus took the bridle and with gentle words encouraged the sturdy pony to walk on.

The sun was setting as they reached a large village and there, by the wayside, was an inn.

Gaius climbed down stiffly from the cart and helped his wife to descend then he went into the inn to ask for a room.

"We want a room for the night and stabling for the horse. Our slave will sleep in the stables if possible or in the cart, and we want dinner for all of us."

Verina inspected the room and Gaius went with Paulus to ensure that the cart and its contents would be safe during the night, then the three of them sat in the main room of the inn where they were served with a plain but copious meal. Cornelia shared the bedchamber with her parents, a thing she did not ever remember doing before, but in spite of her father's snoring she slept like a log after her day spent in the open.

Next day they set off again as soon as they had broken their fast. The day was not as fair as the first but although the sky was not as blue and occasionally looked a little threatening it did not rain. As they got nearer to Londinium they passed through an increasing number of villages until they eventually arrived at a bridge that spanned the biggest river Cornelia had ever seen. There were many carts, both loaded and empty, crossing in both directions and the river itself was busy with all manner of craft. Alongside the wharves there were boats that were bigger than Cornelia ever imagined a boat could be.

Paulus guided their pony and cart over the bridge through the traffic and they entered the city. Cornelia's eyes were wide with amazement at all she saw. The streets were busy with people, even at this late hour, and as they drove into a wide square there were people crying out their wares and selling all manner of things. Paulus turned the cart into a side street and stopped before an inn. Once more Gaius went in to negotiate with the landlord. This one came out and Gaius pulled back the cover on the cart and the man inspected the produce they had brought with them.

"I'll take a haunch of pork and two cheeses and two boxes of apples in exchange for the lodging," he said. "Your slave can take the cart through to the yard and he'll find one of my boys to help with the horse. The cart can go in the woodshed and your slave can sleep with my slaves."

Paulus and Gaius went through to the yard at the back and a boy rushed forward to help with the horse. They unharnessed the horse and he was led to a stall where he was fed and watered. The three then pushed the cart into the shed at the back and the landlord came out to collect the agreed victuals.

"You can share my quarters," said the boy to Paulus.

"Thank you," said Paulus politely. "I'll see what my master says."

The boy carried a haunch of pork towards the back door of the inn and while he was out of earshot Paulus said

"I think it would be best if I sleep in the cart until all the produce is sold, Master."

"Very wise. I'll see to it that your dinner is brought to you."

"Thank you, Master."

Cornelia was given a separate room from her parents. It wasn't exactly a room, more a space under the eves that was curtained off from the main passage. It contained no more than a bed but there was a dormer window that looked out over the yard. She dumped her bedding on the bed and went in search of the latrine. She found this at the side of the yard then went in to take her place at table. The food was in some ways familiar and in others strange to her. She did not like the strange shellfish that were called oysters but the meat roasted with herbs was delicious. There was a pie that contained some sort of fowl and the aroma that rose as the crust was broken was enticing. A bowl of apples appeared on the table and a generous wedge of cheese, both of which she recognised as having come from home. There was also a platter with a beautiful bunch of purple grapes. She had tasted grapes before but they were a rare commodity in her part of the country so she regaled herself with these.

"Can we go out after dinner and look at the city?" she asked.

"I don't think so," said her mother.

"No," said her father. "By the time we've finished it will be getting dark and as we don't know our way about too well we could get lost. Apart from that it's probably dangerous. No, we'll go to bed early and go out in the morning."

Cornelia felt frustrated but knew it was no use arguing with her father. After dinner they went to their beds and Cornelia lay for a while listening to the unfamiliar sounds of the city until she fell asleep.

She was awoken by a sunbeam shining in her face from the window. As she came to her senses she remembered where she was and scrambled to her knees on the bed. She leaned her elbows on the windowsill and looked down into the yard. Paulus came out of the latrine in the corner and walked over to the well in the centre of the yard. He let the bucket down into the depths and she heard the chain rattle. He pulled up the full pail and stood it on the low wall around the well. He then took off his tunic and sandals and standing mother naked in the early morning sunlight he washed himself all over and finished by pouring the last of the water over his head. He dried himself vigorously with a rough piece of linen cloth and donned his clothes again. Cornelia did not find his nakedness embarrassing. As children they had often frolicked naked in the swimming place in the river. But since she had become a woman they had not swum together and she was strangely moved when she saw how his body had changed since those days. His previously scrawny body was sturdy and muscular and his sex had grown since she last saw it and it nestled in a bushy patch of brown hair. Eventually the call of nature forced her to leave her little window and pulling on her dress she made her way down to the latrine. On her way back she encountered the innkeeper's wife and asked for water to be brought for her morning toilet. She washed herself and combed her own hair then descended once more to the tavern room. She found it deserted at this early hour but a slave was busy in the next room preparing the tables for the morning collation.

Cornelia looked out into the street. It was not very wide but it was already abustle with people. They all seemed to be going in the same direction and Cornelia strolled along to the corner of the street to see where they were all going. Most of them turned left and through an archway Cornelia could see an open space full of people setting up stalls and shouting to one another with their slightly odd accent. She was about to go and investigate when a hand took hold of her elbow and Paulus's voice said,

"And where do you think you're going?"

"I want to go into that square, it looks like a gigantic market."

"You can't. A lady cannot walk about alone, who knows what might happen to you, and no one would know where you were. It's lucky that I spotted you going down the street. I don't suppose you told anyone of your plans."

Cornelia was annoyed at having been thwarted.

"I didn't have any plans," she said crossly. "I just wanted to see the town."

"Come back now and after we have broken our fast I'm sure we'll all go and see the town."

Cornelia was annoyed at having been checked by a slave but she decided to return to the inn with him. She strode ahead with her head held high and Paulus sensed her frustration in each step she took. He smiled gently to himself and walked a pace or so behind her. People looked admiringly at this lovely girl, with her head of curls like burnished copper held proudly erect as she walked along with her slave in attendance, but she was too cross to notice the admiring glances. They reached the door of the inn and before Paulus went round to the stable yard Cornelia turned to him and said softly

"Please don't tell father."

"I won't, but please don't go wandering unattended."

"I won't," she replied, and went in in search of her parents.

Later that morning she had her wish. They were going to the forum. She walked along between her parents and Paulus walked behind. The street in which their inn was situated was narrow and the buildings cut out the sunlight. Although Cornelia had walked almost to the end of it earlier nothing had prepared her for the sight that met her eyes as they stepped into the forum. The square was bigger than any she had ever seen and was surrounded by buildings much larger than their inn, larger, even, than their villa at home. To one side of the square was an immense building with two floors. Her father told her it was the Basilica. On the other three sides were shops and offices. The shutters of the shops were all down and through the open fronts one could see the many goods displayed for sale. There were fabrics of more colours than Cornelia had ever imagined, there were shoes, there was jewellery, there were tools, there were pots of all sizes, there were workshops making furniture and eating houses with tables and benches for the customers and delicious aromas came from their depths. In the square itself there were stalls selling vegetables and fruit. There were sausage sellers and cake sellers. There was a stall selling drinks of colourful syrups. There were plump matrons with pink arms selling eggs and yellow cheeses. The whole was a huge medley of sounds and smells and people.

"Mother, look at those wonderful fabrics, and those sandals, and what a pretty cosmetics box. Oh father, this is wonderful. Thank you for bringing us. It will take all day to see everything here."

Her father laughed at her innocent excitement and said "I expect it will, but first I have to see about selling our produce."

Gaius looked around at the various stalls and approached a stall selling fruit. He spoke to the proprietor and an agreement was struck over the apples they had brought from home. The remaining cheeses and ham had been sold to the innkeeper who had agreed to take them in payment for their board and lodgings. The business concluded the little party made their way around the square looking with interest at all the things on offer. They stopped at a shop selling jewellery and Gaius offered to buy both his women, as he put it, an item of their choice. Verina chose a pair of gold and enamel brooches to fasten on the shoulders of her robe and Cornelia chose a string of amber beads the colour of dark honey. She hung them around her neck and admired the effect in the polished mirror that the jeweller held up for her.

"They are lovely," she said and her eyes sparkled. "Thank you father," and she flung her arms around his neck and planted a kiss firmly on each cheek

They walked on around the square and Verina bought some lengths of cloth to make clothes for all her family. She also purchased two fairly large cooking pots and a smaller pot of bronze. Paulus took all these purchases as he followed behind. After a while Gaius turned to him and said,

"You can go and see the fruit seller now. His slave will come with you back to the inn to collect the apples. Leave our purchases in our bedchamber and come back with him with the apples. The fruiterer will pay you."

"Yes master. Where will you be?"

"We will be in that eating-house on the corner. Take some of the money to buy yourself a sausage or something for your meal."

"Thank you master," and hoisting his burden onto his shoulder Paulus strode off in the direction of the fruit stall.

Gaius, Verina and Cornelia seated themselves in front of the eating-house under a canvas awning that was suspended from above the counter. The proprietor brought them three thick tumblers of wine and water and asked them if they would like roast chicken or mutton stew for their main course. They enjoyed the food but all agreed that the food from home tasted better. After the meat course the proprietor placed a dish of fruit on the table and a plate of tiny sweetmeats. These were little dumplings stuffed with chopped nuts and dripping with yellow honey. Cornelia had never tasted anything so delicious.

"Mother, can't we have these at home? They are lovely."

"I'll see what we can do. They are nice, but I wouldn't like them every day."

After their meal they continued with their exploration of the forum. They went into the Basilica and admired the mosaics and marvelled at the vastness of the hall. Outside they saw a notice chalked up on a board announcing chariot races that were to be held outside the main city near the fort.

"Can we go?" said Cornelia excitedly.

"We'll see," said her mother.

Cornelia knew from experience that this usually meant that the eventual answer would be "No" so she did what she always did when her mother said "We'll see" and turned to her father.

"Father, pleeeese can we go? I've never seen chariot races."

"I expect so," said her father with a smile. He always found it hard to refuse his beautiful daughter.

"Thank you father," she said elatedly and put her arm around his middle in a hug.

At that point Paulus came up to them and handed Gaius a sum of money.

"Here's the payment for the apples, master."

The quartet continued their excursion by going out of the forum into a side street where they found the workshop of a leather worker. They looked with interest at the goods on sale. Gaius and Paulus were admiring a finely stitched saddle while the two ladies fingered a selection of purses.

"Mother, why don't we buy this for Jo? He needs a new purse."

"That's a good idea, we'll do that."

The purchase was made and they strolled on. They took a circuitous route back towards the river and came upon a public baths. A notice informed them that two days later it would be a "ladies only" day and Verina and Cornelia decided they would like to attend.

Another half an hour saw them back at the inn.

Early next morning Paulus left the stable yard leading the pony. He was taking it outside the city to exercise it. Cornelia and her parents had broken their fast and were discussing plans for the day when Paulus returned. He came into the dining room and bade them all "Good morning". He had been out of town towards the military camp and as he galloped the pony across a large expanse of level ground, which the soldiers used for practice, he saw that they were preparing the place for the chariot races. Stands of seats had already been erected and two soldiers were hammering the turning posts into the ground while a group of about six others was busy sweeping the ground clear of obstacles and strewing clean sand. On his return to town he stopped and asked one of the soldiers at what hour the event would commence. He advised the family that the first races were due to start at the fifth hour.

Paulus led the way out of town and towards the practice ground. He jostled his way through the noisy crowds and found places in the stands. Cornelia was seated between her mother and Paulus and though they were not in the front row they had an excellent view of the proceedings. First the soldiers from the garrison paraded wearing their full armour and carrying shields and arms. Their helmets shone in the sunlight and the plumes nodded. Next came a group of tumblers somersaulting and vaulting over one another. Then two beautiful young boys in simple loin cloths, their bodies covered with some sort of golden cosmetic and wearing golden laurel wreathes on their heads. They were followed by a band of musicians playing merrily and last of all came the garrison commander riding a magnificent horse the like of which Cornelia had never seen. It was so much more elegant and graceful that the ponies she was used to but it pranced with great spirit.

"What a beautiful horse!" she said.

"It's from Arabia," said Paulus, and she wondered how he knew.

The Commander reined in before a man in a sumptuous toga who was sitting in a front row seat at the centre of the stand. The rider saluted this man and as the procession left the arena the dignitary stood up. While Cornelia was watching the procession she had not noticed that more soldiers had wheeled a wooden contraption onto the race course and horses harnessed to chariots were lined up behind, their drivers standing in the chariots, the reins clasped in one hand and a small whip in the other. The dignitary raised his hand in which he was holding a piece of white linen which he held aloft for a moment and then dropped. At the signal the gates sprang open and the horses leaped out and flew down the arena. The crowds started shouting and cheering and there was a great jostling for space by the charioteers as they rounded the turning post. The gates had been removed by the time they completed the first circuit and by now the race was being hotly fought by three chariots. Two had collided and come to grief at the first post and were carted off by soldiers. By the third circuit only two riders were in contention and as one gained on the other by inches the crowd became noisier and noisier and Cornelia found herself jumping up and down in her seat with excitement. A winner was declared and there was a lull while the course was cleared and the gates were set up for another race.

Gaius sent Paulus to go and buy some sausages and he returned with four large sausages, some pears and a small amphora of wine. He passed the food to Verina, who distributed it, and the wine to Gaius who, after he had taken a draught, passed it along for the others to do likewise. Mid afternoon the racing was over and the crowds started to disperse.

"Father, that was one of the most exciting days of my life," said Cornelia. "Thank you."

Gaius and his little family made their way back to their inn. When they arrived back Verina said she was going to have a rest for a while and Gaius said he would take Paulus with him and they would go to the baths.

"What can I do?" said Cornelia

"You could have a rest," said her mother.

"I'm not tired."

"You could read."

This suggestion did not seem very enticing either. Eventually she decided she would ask the innkeeper's wife if she could have some warm water to wash her hair. Her parents found this acceptable and they all went their separate ways. Cornelia went in search of the landlady. In the tavern she saw a girl about the same age as herself. She thought it must be a slave but was not sure.

"Could I have some warm water to wash my hair, please?" she asked politely.

"Yes," said the girl. "I'd love to do it for you; I've been admiring your hair since you arrived."

"Have you?" said Cornelia, surprised. "I haven't noticed you. I mean I haven't noticed you noticing me."

They both laughed.

"I usually help mother in the kitchen when the inn is busy. I saw you through the door."

"Is your father the inn-keeper?" asked Cornelia. "Your life must be very interesting, always meeting new people."

"I suppose one might think so, but last year I went to the country to help look after my mother's sister who was ill with her latest baby and I must say I like the life in the country better. Do you live in the country?"

"Yes, in a villa some days journey southwest of here. I suppose it is quite nice," and she thought of the orchard and the meadow and the bathing pool and the wild flowers. She compared the spaciousness of her home with the tiny rooms in the inn and wondered what it was like to live there in the winter when the days were short and cold. The inn had no hypocaust; the only heat probably came from the kitchen fires.

The girl went into the kitchen and came back with a

wooden pail of warm water and a jug that looked as if it contained beer.

"What's in the jug?"

"It's beer, mother brews it."

"What's it for?"

"To put on your hair."

"Why?"

"It makes it shine. Come to my room and we'll do it there."

Cornelia followed her newfound friend up the stairs to the corridor where she had her bed but instead of turning left she turned right.

At the other end of the corridor was a low door that opened into a small room under the eves. The room was furnished with a low bed and an oak chest. On the wall behind the door were a number of wooden pegs from which various garments were hanging. In a corner was a little tripod holding a basin.

"What a cosy little room," said Cornelia.

"It's not bad. It's nice in winter because it's over the kitchen so it's nice and warm. Would you like to slip the top of your robe down so we don't get it wet and put your head over the basin?"

Cornelia did as she was bid and her hair was washed and then rinsed with the jug of beer. This smelt rather strange but once her head had been well rubbed with towels the smell disappeared.

"I don't know your name," said Cornelia.

"It's Popea," she said.

She made Cornelia sit before the open window so that the sun shone on her head and gradually as Popea combed it it dried to a silky shine.

"That feels lovely, it's so soft."

"You've got lovely curls; let me arrange them for you."

Popea had a definite knack where hairdressing was concerned and when she had finished and she showed Cornelia her reflection in her hand mirror Cornelia was amazed. The hair was all lifted off the nape of her neck and curls were arranged in a cascading bunch on the crown of her head. A few wispy curls played around her temples and the whole creation was mystically held in place by Cornelia's own hair ribbon cleverly threaded and tied.

"That's amazing!" said Cornelia. "I never thought I could look like this."

Popea was as pleased with her handiwork as Cornelia was.

"It's not bad, is it?"

"If you did this for all your lady guests the inn would always be full."

"I never thought of that. Not every lady travels with her own slave."

Popea had to go into the kitchen and help with the evening meal so Cornelia thanked her again and decided to go and decide what to wear for dinner in honour of her new hairstyle. As she was going out of the door she said,

"Oh, that's a shame."

"What is?" asked Popea.

"Mother and I are going to the baths tomorrow so my hair will be ruined."

"That's nice. I'm going to the baths tomorrow with my mother; we always go on the fourth day. Father looks after the tavern. We can go together. My slave can look after you too.

Cornelia went down the corridor to her little alcove and decided to change for dinner. She put on her pale green robe and fastened her string of amber beads around her neck. She descended to the yard and in the corner found an elder tree with heavy heads of berries on it. She plucked some and rubbed the juice on her lips to darken them then walked into the inn to await the hour for dinner. At that moment her father and Paulus returned from the baths, both looking pink and relaxed. Her father kissed her cheek and said "You look very pretty tonight," then went up stairs to find Verina.

Paulus stood and gazed at Cornelia as if seeing her for the first time. She smiled at her childhood friend. Suddenly, in a soft voice he said, "You are very beautiful."

He then turned on his heel and quickly left the room. Cornelia was pleased with the effect her new appearance had had so far but wished Paulus had not rushed off like that. She also wished Paulus was not a slave, although she did not know why she wished that.

Her parents came into the room together and they all went into the dining room.

"Your hair is very nice," said her mother. "You seem to be growing into a young lady at last."

"I've always been a lady," retorted Cornelia, "there's never been anything wrong with my manners."

"Your manners have never been in question," said her father, "just your tom-boyish ways."

Cornelia ignored this remark and turning to her mother she said,

"I have made friends this afternoon with the landlord"s daughter; we are about the same age. She and her mother are going to the baths tomorrow and she has suggested we all go along together and share their slave."

"That's kind," said Verina, "it will be nice to go with someone who knows the way and what to do."

Next morning, soon after their light meal, the small party gathered in the tavern room and set off to the baths. The innkeeper's wife, whose name was Rosa, was as friendly as her daughter and she and Verina walked side-by-side chatting like old friends. Behind them walked their daughters who were deep in a discussion about the merits and demerits of different perfumes. Behind them came the little slave. She was about twelve, as far as one could know, and had belonged to this family for as long as she could remember. She had a very vague recollection of another woman whom she supposed was her mother but she did not remember her with any fondness or regret. She only knew that she had been extremely poor and had sold her for a slave in order to survive.

The little party arrived at the baths and Rosa led the way

into the changing room. They all took off their clothes and the slave girl folded them neatly and placed them in one of the little cubicles that were around the room. She then settled herself on the bench to guard their possessions while they walked through to the tepidarium. Rosa had brought some coins in with her that she handed to a girl who, in exchange for the money, rubbed scented oil into Rosa's body and then massaged it with firm, capable strokes. She then scraped off the oil and washed her body with warm water. The others received the same treatment. Cornelia, once she had become used to the feeling, found it the most wonderful experience of her life. The oil smelled of roses and the masseuse was good at her job.

"Mother, this is wonderful. We must get Florens to do this for us when we go home."

"Do you have baths where you live?" asked Popea.

"No, not like this. We have our own bath-house."

Popea seemed impressed by this information.

"Is there a forum near you?" she asked.

"No, we live in the countryside. There is a small town not too far away that has a market. I go there sometimes with father or Jo when they go to sell the produce."

"Who's Jo?"

"Jovianus, he's my brother."

"I wish I had a brother. I did have two sisters but they both died of the fever a couple of years ago. I got sick too but I recovered. Have you ever had the fever?"

"No, but I remember having the rash when I was little. Mother nursed me herself. I was ill for about a fortnight but I got better."

"Obviously," said Popea, and they laughed.

The massages all finished they went through to the caldarium where they plunged into a bath of hot water. The younger women soon found this boring and Popea said

"Shall we go to the swimming bath? Can you swim?"

"Yes, we swim in the river at home."

They ran through to the swimming bath and both jumped in with great splashing and shouts. After swimming up and down a few times they climbed out and sat on the side.

"Do you have a lover?" asked Popea.

"No, do you?"

"No, but I think father is going to arrange a marriage with someone soon."

"Who?"

"I think it's the son of a friend of his. His father is a wine merchant. He has a warehouse down by the river."

"Do you know him?"

"Yes."

"Do you like him?"

"I think so. He's not very good looking, but he's very kind."

"I wouldn't like to marry anyone ugly. Imagine having to sleep with them. Ughh!"

"He's not ugly, just ordinary. Mother says although it seems nice and romantic to marry someone good looking, looks don't last for very long, but kindness of character does, so I suppose I shall be happy."

"Well I shall make sure I marry someone beautiful," said Cornelia.

"Have you ever been kissed?" asked Popea.

"Not properly, but there is someone I'd like to be kissed by."

"Who? said Popea with great interest.

"He's called Marcus and he's the most beautiful man I've ever seen. He's got brown curly hair and dark twinkly eyes."

"What does he do?"

"He's a soldier, an officer. A real Roman, from Rome."

"But they are not allowed to get married."

"I don't want to get married; I want to see lots of things."

At this point they were joined by their mothers.

"Who would like something to eat?" asked Verina, smiling.

"Yes please," said both the girls.

Verina handed them each a piping hot sausage they had bought from a stall in the atrium and Rosa placed a napkin with a selection of sweetmeats on it on the bench by the wall. The two matrons sat on the bench and the girls sat on the floor at their feet.

"This is good," said Cornelia as she sank her teeth into her sausage and took a bite.

Verina smiled at her daughter.

"I must say getting you to eat your food has never been a problem. I don't know why you're not as fat as butter."

"Unlike me," said Rosa, and grasped the roll of fat around her belly.

"I don't know why I'm not as skinny as an eel. I don't get time to eat too much and I'm on my feet from dawn till dusk. Running an inn is not exactly a relaxing job."

When they had finished eating Rosa returned the napkin to the sweet seller and they all trooped back to the changing room. Rosa handed the slave girl a sausage and she ate it hungrily while they donned their clothes.

That evening, while eating their meal, they told Gaius about the baths.

"What did you do while we were at the baths? asked Verina.

"I made a few purchases."

"I thought you didn't like shopping," said Cornelia.

"It wasn't your kind of shopping," he replied. "I bought some very good wine from a wine merchant that our landlord introduced me to and one or two tools for the farm."

After dinner Verina said "We must all go to our beds early because we will be starting off very early in the morning. I will go and speak to Rosa about food for the journey."

"I'll come with you mother. I want to say "good bye" to Popea, and Rosa of course."

Popea was sitting on a stool in the kitchen eating a plate of stew while Rosa was already packing food for the journey next morning. She was filling Verina's basket with all sorts of things. There was a crusty loaf and a wedge of yellow cheese.

There was a shiny pie and some apples and pears. Carefully wrapped in a linen square was a fine bunch of grapes. The whole was accompanied by a small flask of wine and water.

"I'll put the provisions in the meat safe until the morning," said Rosa.

"Thank you, you've been very kind. Gaius will pay you before he goes to bed."

"It's been a pleasure. I don't often get the company of another woman. Mostly my guests are merchants."

Popea placed her now empty plate on the table and came over to Cornelia.

"Good bye, and thank you for your company."

"Thank you for doing my hair, and for taking us to the baths, I've really enjoyed London."

"I hope we'll see you all again one day."

Chapter Three

Noon some days later saw them driving through the gate into the yard at the side of the villa. As Cornelia jumped down from the cart she was greeted by an ecstatic Hector who leaped and yelped around her feet. She bent to fondle his head and he licked her face vigorously. His tail wagged so much his whole rear end was wriggling to and fro then he suddenly took off at top speed through the orchard, down to the stream and back again. At last he settled down by her feet, his pink tongue lolling to the side and what looked like a grin on his face. Jovianus came striding into the yard and greeted the travellers.

"Hello," he said, and hugging his mother and stroking Cornelia's hair he added, "it's nice to see you home. Did you have a good journey, and did you enjoy Londinium?"

"It was wonderful," said Cornelia. "The shops were wonderful and the buildings were wonderful and the baths were wonderful, and we went to the races and they were – well, wonderful."

Everyone laughed and Verina gathered together some of her parcels and handing some to Cornelia she said,

"Help me carry these in. Jo can bring the rest."

Cornelia went into her room and found Florens waiting for her.

"Hello Florens," she said.

"Hello my lady. Did you have a good trip?"

"It was wonderful. I saw so many things. I made friends with the innkeeper's daughter and she showed me how to dress my hair in a very stylish fashion. I'll teach you so you can do it for me; and we went to the public baths and mother and I both had a massage. We saw huge buildings and we saw the races and we ate grapes almost every day. But I missed some of our food from home."

As she talked Florens was unpacking her baggage and admired the string of amber beads. Cornelia undressed and Florens poured water from a pitcher into a basin so she could wash before dinner. She set out a fresh tunic on the bed and when Cornelia was ready she combed her hair for her.

"Here," said Cornelia, "I've got some hairpins to pin my hair up on top. You have to twist it into curls and pin them on top of my head and then put a ribbon round so they don't fall down."

"Like this?" said Florens, and after one or two attempts she succeeded in creating a passable reproduction of the style that Popea had created.

"Yes, that's not bad."

Then she put her amber beads on and sat whilst Florens fastened her sandals. Hector was sitting almost on her feet and licked her toes. As soon as she rose and left the room he walked along as if glued to her legs. He was not going to let his adored mistress out of his sight ever again.

She went to the dining room but none of the family was there yet. She asked one of the slaves who was preparing the table to pour her a cup of wine and water and she sat down to wait. Hector knew that the dining room was forbidden him and he lay just outside the doorway in the passage watching her. Soon her brother came in.

"Move out of the way dog, don't lie in the passageway."

Hector moved about a foot to the side but refused to go away. Jovianus saw Cornelia and said,

"My, don't you look elegant. I think you might be growing up at last."

Cornelia blushed at the compliment. It was not the sort of remark her brother ever made.

"I'm perfectly grown up," she answered, and took another sip of her wine. "Has anything happened while we were away?"

What she really wanted to say was "Have you seen Marcus?" but she did not want to let her brother know that she was interested in him.

"The brown mare had her foal, a nice healthy animal, and we've harvested the pears and laid them in the store. They are good this year. The wheat is ready and if this dry weather holds we shall start harvesting tomorrow, we needed Paulus and the other cart."

Cornelia really was not interested in pears and wheat and carts, though she determined to go and see the new foal next morning. She was saved from further conversation of an agricultural nature by the entry of her parents and two slaves bearing steaming dishes. She attacked her food with her usual appetite but after dinner, when her father and brother retired to the study to discuss estate business her mother said,

"I shall go to bed early tonight; I'm rather tired after the journey. Good night. Sleep well."

Cornelia decided that the thought of her own bed in her own room was very attractive and in fact, although she insisted to herself that she was not tired, she was asleep almost as soon as her head was down.

The fine weather did hold and two days later Cornelia decided to go into the fields and pick blackberries. She called Hector and the two of them set off up the rutted lane from the villa. She sang as she walked along, swinging a basket and Hector ran too and fro chasing exciting smells in the hedgerows. She soon gathered a good supply of fruit and leaving the field she was in she made her way to the top of a nearby hill. The hill was crowned with a stand of trees and in the centre lay a large stone. People said that once it was standing upright but the tree roots had undermined it and it had fallen over. It now afforded a convenient seat from which one obtained a wonderful view over the surrounding countryside. As she approached the top of the hill Hector gave a little yelp and ran off excitedly. Cornelia thought he had no doubt found the scent of a hare but was surprised to see Marcus, sitting on the ground with his back to the stone. His horse was loosely tied to a branch and was nuzzling amongst the undergrowth looking for grass. Hector had run up to Marcus, whom he obviously recognised, and was greeting him energetically.

"Hello," said Cornelia, surprised. Her heart had started to beat faster and she was sure she had gone red.

"Hello," said Marcus, jumping to his feet, and they stood and looked at one another a trifle awkwardly. Then they both spoke at once and they laughed and broke the spell.

"I didn't expect to see you here," said Cornelia.

"I often come here," said Marcus. "It's a good resting place after a ride before turning back. I'm exercising the horse. Won't you sit down?"

Cornelia went and sat on the stone and placed her basket on the ground. Marcus sat beside her, but not too close.

"I see you've been blackberrying," he said. "You've got juice stains around your mouth."

Cornelia wiped her hand over her mouth with little effect.

"Here, let me," said Marcus and taking a square of red linen from around his neck he offered a corner and said

"Lick."

She obediently licked the cloth and he rubbed the stains from her face.

"Thank you," she said.

"You have a very beautiful mouth," he said, and his hand stayed suspended before her lips. She felt herself reddening under his gaze. He replaced his neck square without taking his eyes from her face. There was another awkward silence then Marcus restored normality by saying,

"What did you think of London?"

Cornelia quickly regained her usual demeanour and answered enthusiastically,

"It was wonderful. How did you know I had been there?"

"Your brother told me."

"Of course. It was very exciting. We went to the chariot racing and to the baths. The shops were marvellous and father bought me some beautiful amber beads. I would like to go there again one day, I'm sure there's a lot more to see."

"I'm sure there is, but if you like cities you should see Rome."

"Have you been to Rome?"

"Yes, that's my home."

"Tell me about it."

"Well, it's much bigger than Londinium, but it's on a river just the same. The buildings are beautiful and the sun shines nearly every day."

"What sort of buildings? Are there baths?"

"Oh yes, huge baths, very well appointed. Dozens of temples, of course, the Forum for business, the Circus Maxiumus for festivals – and there's an amphitheatre that would probably hold most of the people in London at once."

"Ye Gods!" exclaimed Cornelia. "And what are the houses like?"

"Well, the rich people have beautiful villas but quite a lot of people live in insulae, lots of apartments in one big building."

"Do you live in an apartment or in a villa?"

"We have an apartment."

Suddenly Cornelia's thoughts came down with a jolt. Who was "we"?

"Who's we?" she asked. "Do you have a wife in Rome?"

"No, I'm not allowed to have a wife while I'm in the army. I live with my mother and my sister, when I'm at home. My mother owns the insula. My father died and left it to her. That's how we live."

"I see. Is it very big?"

"Fairly. There are shops on the ground floor and apartments on the other four floors."

"Four!"

"Yes," he laughed.

"How old is your sister?"

"Sixteen."

"What does she do?"

"She helps mother with the tenants. She does all sorts of things."

"What sort of things?"

"She helps to record the money. She shows people around when they want to rent an apartment. She makes sure the slaves keep the stairs and passages clean. Lots of things."

"Does she have any friends?"

"Oh yes. They go to the market together and to the baths. They go to the games and the races. The house always seems to be overflowing with at least half a dozen of them, all trying on robes and doing one another's hair and chattering like a cageful of parakeets."

"It sounds nice. I wish I could go to Rome."

"I expect you will one day."

Marcus rose to his feet and taking her hand he pulled her up. The feeling of his hand on hers gave her that strange feeling low down in her belly again.

"Come on, I'll walk part of the way with you."

He untethered his horse and leading it by the bridle walked by Cornelia's side till they reached the lane.

"Here's where we part," he said.

"Will you be coming to the hill stone again?"

"I expect so, if the weather's fair. I exercise the horse nearly every day."

"I'll see you there again, then."

"Sure to. Farewell pretty lady," and he mounted his horse with one strong movement and rode off down the lane.

Cornelia turned towards home and with Hector at her heels she walked up the lane with the sensation that she was floating above the ground.

The next day it rained. Cornelia wandered disconsolately around the house and outbuildings. She went to see how the new foal was getting on. It was a lovely colour, not unlike her own hair, and it had a bushy little tail that twitched as he suckled. She went to her room and spent time looking through her clothes and arranging her hair in different styles. She then decided to go and spend time in the bath, so gathering together a linen towel, a bottle of scented oil and various implements she called Florens and made her way through the rain to the bathhouse. After Florens had oiled and scraped her body she went through to the small room where the hot tub was situated and sank herself into the very warm water. She rolled up her towel to make a pillow and putting it on the edge of the bath she laid her head back and relaxed. She thought about Marcus and wondered what he was doing. She thought about what it would be like when he kissed her, for he definitely would kiss her. She thought of the way his mouth wrinkled at the corners when he smiled and how his brown eyes twinkled when he spoke to her. She thought of his straight, slender body and muscular legs and imagined being pressed up against him, and then there was that strange fluttering low down in her belly again. Having lived all her life surrounded by nature and farm animals she was not ignorant of conception and birth. She knew that one day this would be her lot just as it was for the mare that had just foaled and the cows and sheep. It held no fear for her. But she was completely ignorant about what went on between a couple before pregnancy. She did not believe that a husband merely mounted his wife in order to procreate like the farm animals. She was sure there was more to it that that. She had been friendly with a girl who lived on a neighbouring farm and they used to talk for hours about the things that were happening to their developing bodies and speculating about just what went on when you were married. This girl was a year older than Cornelia and she had married the previous year. Cornelia waited excitedly to meet her again after her wedding to learn exactly what went on but when they did meet again her friend seemed changed and though she chatted about clothes and a trip she had made to the nearest market she was reluctant to discuss the secrets of the marriage bed and Cornelia did not know how to ask her.

Florens interrupted her reverie by poking her head round the doorway to announce that dinner was nearly ready.

Cornelia climbed out of the bath and Florens, taking a pailful of cold water, splashed her quickly to cool her down then rubbed her body vigorously with the towel. Cornelia threaded her head through the neck of her tunic and as she was pinning the shoulders Florens slipped her sandals onto her feet for her and fastened them.

She walked into the dining room just as the food was being served.

"This rain is a nuisance," said her brother. "I wanted to harvest the top field today. Now it will have to wait until it dries off again."

"I think it will be dry again tomorrow. The clouds have cleared and it looks as if there's going to be a good sunset."

"I hope so," said Cornelia. "I don't like rainy days."

Gaius's predictions were correct and the next day dawned bright and clear and the world had been washed by the previous day's rain. In the middle of the morning she called to her mother, "I'm going out for a walk," and calling Hector she set off along the lane. As she neared the hill where the fallen stone lay Hector bounded off with a happy yelp and as she reached the top of the hill she saw him greeting Marcus gleefully. Marcus picked up a stick and threw it for Hector to retrieve.

"He'll let you do that for him all day," said Cornelia.

"Hello, I'm glad you came."

"I'm glad you were here."

"Shall we walk?"

"Yes, that would be nice. What about the horse?"

"Oh he's all right."

They walked down the other side of the hill along a pathway that bore hoof prints of Marcus's horse and then turned into the woodland at the bottom. Some of the trees were already taking on their autumn colours and their feet rustled through a covering of fallen leaves on the ground. Marcus climbed over a fallen tree in the way and turning offered his hand to help Cornelia over. As she jumped down the other side he kept her hand in his and Cornelia felt the vigour of his body flowing between their palms. Marcus smiled down at her then he turned and taking her gently in his arms he put his lips gently on hers. Suddenly that funny little flicker in her belly burst into flame and she strained her body towards his. The kiss lasted a long time then Marcus gently put her from him and said,

"Sorry, I didn't really mean to do that."

"Didn't you? I did," said Cornelia.

She looked round and saw Hector sitting down looking at them with his head on one side and his pink tongue hanging out. Cornelia laughed at him and his tail thumped on the ground.

"Hector didn't mind," she said, laughing.

"It's not Hector I'm worried about."

"Then what?"

"Your father, your mother and probably your brother. I shouldn't like to have to fight him."

Cornelia laughed.

"Why would Jo want to fight you? Jo never fights."

"He might feel obliged to fight to protect his sister."

"From what?"

"From me. You are the most exciting girl I have ever met. I wanted you from the moment I set eyes on you."

"I want you, too."

"That's the problem. I'm a soldier and as such I am not allowed to marry. It's another twelve years before I retire and get my land and can take a wife."

"That's very unfair."

"Perhaps, but it's the way it is. I can't expect you to wait for me for twelve more years."

Cornelia looked crestfallen.

"But I love you. I don't want to wait twelve years before I marry, and I don't want anyone else."

Hand in hand they walked slowly back to the horse.

"I think it would be better if we don't meet for a while."

"Don't any soldiers have wives and families? Supposing you became a soldier after you got married, what then?"

Lots of men have families but they have to put the army first and that is not a life for you."

"I don't care."

"But I do. You are special. I won't do it."

He kissed her very gently on the lips and mounted his horse. Cornelia watched him ride away with tears in her eyes. Then she swore loudly and kicked a clump of wild flowers.

Hector jumped out of her way and looked at her from a distance. She walked home slowly thinking how unfair life was.

The following week two things happened that were to change her life forever. The first event was that her mother called her one morning and said, "We are having a guest for dinner today. I want you to wear your best robe and get Florens to arrange your hair. I want you to be on your best behaviour and exercise some charm, for your father's sake."

Cornelia did as she was bid, wondering who the guest was to be and whether her father was trying to impress him to accomplish a business arrangement.

Cornelia walked into the dining room looking demure and very pretty. The guest was already there talking with her father and brother. It was Crassus, the son of the owner of an estate about ten miles away. He was about the same age as Jo but could not have been more different. His hair was sparse, fair and straight. His eyes were a watery blue and his lips somehow managed to look always wet. He was tall enough but walked with a stoop, as if he were permanently bowing to someone.

"Ah, here is my daughter," said Gaius. "I imagine it must be some time since you met."

"It certainly is. She could have been no more than ten or eleven last time I saw her. I must say there has been a considerable improvement," and he smiled in a way that Cornelia could only describe as smarmy. As he spoke she smelt his bad breath and saw that quite a few of his teeth were black.

She remembered what her mother had told her about charming their guest and said how nice it was to see him again. She asked after his parents.

"Unfortunately my father went to his rest last winter."

"I'm sorry to hear that. How is your mother?"

"She's coping quite well. I am in charge of the estate now. My sisters are both married and no longer live at home."

At this point her mother came in followed by slaves with the first course and the dinner proceeded. Her parents took over the conversation and Cornelia took the opportunity to look at Crassus while they ate. She could not find fault with his table manners but he made noises when he ate and as he emptied his wine goblet he became more garrulous and red in the face.

When the savoury courses were finished and cleared away the slaves brought in a large platter of fruit and a dish of the little sweet dumplings swimming in honey that they had had in London. Crassus helped himself to a generous portion of these and proclaimed them delicious.

"Almost as sweet as your sweet daughter, but not quite," he said. He licked his thin lips and his tongue reminded Cornelia of a snake. She had lost count of how much wine he had drunk.

Eventually Crassus announced that he must take his leave, as his mother would no doubt be worried about him being out late. Jovianus went out of the room to tell the slaves that their guest was ready to leave and instructed them to inform his own slave and bring the horses to the front of the house. They all congregated in the atrium to say their goodbyes and Cornelia heaved a sigh of relief when the door was shut on the departing riders.

"I congratulate you," said Verina to her daughter. "You look very nice and you behaved perfectly."

"Well, I hope that whatever it is that father is trying to arrange with him is successful. I think I should like to go to bed now."

"Very well dear. Sleep well. Good night."

Next morning at breakfast her mother said,

"Crassus is a very wealthy man now that his father is gone."

"I expect he is," said Cornelia, and served herself with a dish of apples cooked in honey.

Her father came into the room and took the place opposite her.

"What did you think of our guest last night?" he asked Cornelia.

"He was polite enough, but I think he drank more wine than he needed."

"You know he is now a very wealthy man. His farm and villa are much bigger than ours."

"I suppose they are," said Cornelia, noncommittally.

"Do you know why he came last night?"

"I assumed he had some sort of business proposal to put to you."

"In a way he did. He wants to marry you."

Cornelia looked as if she had been struck by lightening. Her spoon stopped in mid air and her mouth remained open to receive the food that never arrived.

"What do you think?" said her father.

For the first time in ages Cornelia was stuck for words. She placed her spoon on her plate and stared at her parents.

"What do I think? I think he's revolting. I never liked him when we were children and I like him less now. He's creepy and his breath stinks."

Her parents looked at her and then at each other. Her father looked annoyed but before he could utter her mother spoke.

"I can see that this has come as something of a shock, we don't expect you to agree immediately. Give yourself time, and think it over. You would be the mistress of a very sizeable property. You would have plenty of slaves and Crassus is a very wealthy man. As his wife he would probably refuse you nothing."

"But I don't love him, and he doesn't love me. In fact when we were children he told me he thought I was the bossiest most self-opinionated girl he knew and he hoped I would be married off to some horrid old man who beat me. Anyway, I thought his father wanted him to marry some girl from Venta Belgarum as part of a business deal."

Verina laughed.

"Well, I can assure you that his opinion of you has changed; and as to love, well, that is something that comes with marriage. You just have to be patient."

Cornelia could see that arguing with her parents would probably not have the desired effect so she did not stress her point, but she decided that she would have to find some way to convince them that Crassus was not the man for her.

"Is it necessary to make a decision right away?" she asked.

"No, of course not," said her father, relieved that his daughter seemed to be prepared to consider the proposition. "Take as much time as you need to become accustomed to the idea."

"But not too long," said her mother, "he might get impatient and take another bride."

"Very well. I'll think about it."

Cornelia had absolutely no intention of marrying anyone as repulsive as Crassus. The thought of his clammy hands exploring her body made her flesh creep. She did not know what she would do to get out of it but at least she had bought herself time to think. Then the second bombshell dropped.

She was about to go out for a walk when she heard the wheels of a cart turning into the yard. She went out into the garden and looking towards the yard she saw Marcus with another officer and two men. They had come for a load of wheat but since the arrangements had been made Marcus only came from time to time to settle the bill. Usually the men came alone. But this time not only was Marcus here but a second officer.

Jovianus went up to them and bade them good morning and the three went into the house. When the cart was loaded and ready to depart the three came out of the house. They made their formal farewells then Marcus, seeing Cornelia sitting on a bench under an apple tree came over to her.

"Hello," he said, and smiled his heart-stopping smile.

"Hello."

"Will you walk part of the way with me? We could go to the fallen stone."

Cornelia rose without speaking and accompanied him across to the yard gate. They walked along together in silence until they reached the little coppice. They sat down on the stone. The sun had not warmed it yet and it felt cold through her thin tunic

"I have something to tell you," he said.

She looked at him enquiringly.

"I have to say 'Good bye'".

"Why?" she said, her eyes wide.

"My cavalry regiment has been recalled. We are to go back to Rome and take up winter quarters then we are to be sent somewhere else in the spring."

"When are you going?"

"In four days."

"Will I see you before you go?"

"No, I shan't be able to come again; I shall be too busy at camp."

Cornelia's eyes filled with tears then her temper flared and she stood up and stamped her foot on the ground.

"I hate the army."

Marcus stood up and held her in his arms till her rage subsided, then they kissed long and lovingly. He released her and said,

"I must go now. If I hurry I can catch up with the cart.

Please don't be too sad. Get married and have lots of babies."

He tore himself away and started down the path to the track. She watched him go and when he turned to wave he saw that she was sobbing. She saw him regain the track where he broke into a trot and she watched him until he disappeared from view.

Over the next couple of days she was very quiet and thoughtful. Her mother thought she was contemplating the possibility of marriage with Crassus. Little did she know what plans were forming in her daughter's mind.

Cornelia had considered her situation and considered the alternatives. She could refuse to marry Crassus and stay an old maid. She could ask her parents to find her a different husband, one she could at least be friends with. She could run away to London and go and live with Popea and her mother and help at the inn. None of these possibilities seemed attractive. Then, after two days of deep thought she had an idea. She would go to Rome!

Once her mind was made up she became more cheerful and she started to make her plans. She would need money. This was a commodity she had very little of. Not because her parents were mean but because she had no need for it at home. The next day was market day and she begged her father for money and asked Jovianus to allow her to accompany him to the market. She said she wanted to buy some new sandals. She accomplished this task with no trouble and she did, indeed, buy herself some sandals; after all Rome was a long way to walk, but she made sure she spent only a small portion of the cash.

On the evening of the fourth day, the day on which she knew Marcus's unit was leaving, she went to bed as normal. Once the house was quiet and everyone was asleep she took the blanket from her bed and folded it in half lengthways. On it she laid some clothes and her new sandals and rolled it up and tied it with one of her girdles. She took her small store of coins and all her jewellery and put it in a leather bag with a long strap. She took her writing tablet and wrote on it "I will never marry Crassus. I am going to Rome. Do not worry about me."

She placed the tablet on her bed and then gently opening her bedroom door she crept quietly to the kitchen. There she appropriated a loaf of bread, the remains on the fowl they had had for dinner and some fruit. She wrapped the meat in a linen napkin and put it and the bread and fruit in the bag. Hector had followed her to the kitchen in the vain hope that there might be an extra snack somewhere in this unusual adventure. Cornelia saw a mutton bone with some meat left on it and taking this she went back to her room. She called Hector into the room and gave him the bone. While he was engrossed in gnawing this nocturnal gift she shut the door and quietly crept out of the house. She slung her bundle on one shoulder and her bag on the other and set off at a brisk pace down the track.

The night was balmy and there was quite a large moon and she could see the track winding along in front of her. Her spirits were high and she felt a keen sense of adventure. She soon reached the opening of the path that led up to the fallen stone. The trees made it dark and she felt the path was eerie, as if something up there was watching her. She was glad her way took her straight past and on along the lane to the road. On her left a cow snorted in the field and suddenly a fox ran across her path, making her jump.

She reached the road sooner than she expected and hesitated a second as to which way to go. She knew that left led to the track where the army camp was and, eventually, to London. However, she also knew that right led to the sea, and that one had to cross the sea to get to Rome. So she turned right.

She hoped she would soon catch up with Marcus's soldiers who had left that afternoon but the countryside was still and quiet. She made good pace on the metalled road and just as she saw a hint of dawn she caught sight of the army tents and heard slight noises of people. When she arrived at the fringes of the camp she was surprised to see quite a lot of women and children camped on the ground with their bundles of belongings around them. She thought there might possibly be half a dozen or so families following the camp but was surprised to see how many there were. She estimated there must be more than fifty people. She chose a spot under a tree and spreading her blanket on the ground she wrapped herself in her cloak and went to sleep. She would go in search of Marcus in the morning.

The sun was up and the soldiers were already forming into lines to march when she was awakened by a warm tongue licking her face. She opened her eyes to see Hector. His tail was wagging so hard his whole body was undulating and he was giving little yelps of joy.

"Oh Hector, how did you get here?" she said.

She pushed herself up into a sitting position and saw, standing behind Hector, a pair of brown, sturdy legs. She looked up to see who the owner of the legs was. Looking down at her, his hands on his hips, was Paulus.

"Where do you think you're going?"

"I'm going to Rome. Why have you followed me?"

"Your father has sent me to bring you back. Your mother is out of her mind with worry."

"I told her not to worry."

"Of course she'll worry. What did you expect?"

"Well I'm not coming back."

"I promised your father I would find you."

"Well, you've found me. Now go away."

"I can't. What do you think he would do to me if I were to go home without you?"

"I don't care. He wants me to marry Crassus."

"That weed!"

"Yes."

"Well, you can refuse, but you still have to come home."

Cornelia, by now, was standing up and had started gathering her effects together.

"I shan't come home, and you can't make me."

Paulus had to admit to himself that it would be very difficult to make her go home. He could not very well pick her up and carry her back, although the possibility did enter his mind, and even if he did manage to persuade her to return how long would it be before she made another bid for freedom and independence? After all, her parents could not lock her up. Paulus came to a decision.

"Well, I can't let you go off alone; I promised your parents that I would make sure you were unharmed. If you insist on going to Rome I shall have to come with you."

This was a development that Cornelia had not considered, but now that she did it struck her as a good idea. A lady travelling with her own slave would have more respect than a lady travelling alone. Also, she had to admit to herself, it made her feel safer having Paulus to protect her. Paulus thought that this was probably the best way to get her to return. If things did not go as planned, if the weather turned bad, or they were beset by bandits, or plague she might then be glad to go home. She looked at Paulus and said "All right, you can come," then as if she read his thoughts she added, "but I won't turn back."

The troupe of camp followers had gathered themselves together and was ready to take to the road. Paulus shouldered Cornelia's bundle along with his own and they set off down the road side by side with Hector at Cornelia's heels.

The day passed uneventfully and when they stopped for the night Cornelia determined to seek out Marcus.

"I'm just going for a walk," she said to Paulus.

"Where are you going?"

"To the camp. I want to find Marcus."

"Very well," said Paulus, but as soon as she was a short way off he followed her discreetly. When she arrived at the camp she enquired of some soldiers who were digging a trench where she could find Marcus. One of the soldiers stopped digging and indicated with his hand the direction she should take. Paulus could not hear what he said but he continued to follow her. As he drew level with the soldiers he heard one say to the other

"That's a stunning piece of recreation; I wouldn't mind her coming to look for me."

"Mind your tongue," said Paulus.

The soldiers looked at him and decided it would be wiser not to tangle with this sturdy slave, especially as his mistress was obviously connected with their superior officer. The soldier who had spoken grunted an apology and returned to his spadework. Cornelia caught sight of Marcus who was obviously giving instructions about his horse to a soldier. The soldier took the reins and led the horse away. Marcus turned and suddenly caught sight of Cornelia walking towards him. He stopped dead in his tracks and his jaw dropped. It was obvious to Paulus that her presence there was a surprise so he knew that they had not colluded together for her to run away. What Paulus saw next made his heart drop like a stone. She ran up to Marcus and straight into his open arms. They stood for a while with their arms around each other then Marcus put her gently away from him and Paulus heard him say "What on earth are you doing here?"

"I've run away, I'm coming to Rome with you."

"I thought I would never see you again."

"I couldn't bear not to see you again, and when they told me they wanted me to marry Crassus I decided to take matters into my own hands."

"Do your parents know where you are?"

"Oh yes, I left a note."

"They are sure to come after you."

"They did. Well, that is to say they sent Paulus to bring me back, but I won't go so he's coming with me."

"I don't think this is the wisest thing you've ever done, but I don't suppose it will do any good if I tell you I think you ought to go home?"

"No good at all, that is unless you do not want me to go with you?"

"It's not a case of what I want. I have my duty to the army. You are presenting me with something of a problem."

He looked at her with a frown then he said "Oh well, at least you have your slave to protect you, it's a very long way to Rome and I have to stay with my men most of the time. Where are you camping?"

"Just over there, on that little bank at the edge of the trees."

"I'll try and come over later."

"That would be nice."

He looked deep into her eyes and stroked her hair. Then against his better judgement he said "I love you."

"I love you too."

She turned and walked away from him and he called out "See you later".

As she came out of the camp Paulus was waiting to accompany her. She walked alongside him with a look of perfect happiness on her face. When they got back to their chosen camping spot Hector was lying on their bundles guarding them and he thumped his tail as they approached. Paulus spread out their sleeping blankets as Cornelia laid out the food for a meagre supper. They still had some bread but it was now somewhat stale and Paulus had brought some cheese. Cornelia still had a few apples.

"I'll just go to the stream and fetch some water. There's still a little wine in the wineskin."

They were sitting eating their frugal meal when they saw the figure of Marcus coming towards them. He was carrying a small cooking pot from which a wonderful smell drifted to their nostrils.

"I don't know what you had intended for supper. I have brought you some stew."

"That's wonderful," said Cornelia and Marcus placed the pot on the ground between them. Paulus took two spoons from their food bag and he and Cornelia tucked into the pot together. Marcus laughed.

"I can see that marching gives you an appetite."

"Leave some for Hector," said Cornelia. "There's a nice bone in the bottom."

"I'll wash the pot and bring it back to you," said Paulus.

"That's all right, you can keep it, I have another."

"How much further before we get to the sea?" asked Paulus.

"About another day and a half."

"I thought the sea was nearer than that."

"It is but we have to go further along the coast to meet the naval ships."

"How will we get to Gaul?" asked Cornelia.

"You'll be all right. There will be merchant ships there willing to make the crossing to Gaul. It should not cost too much. Ships go back and forth all the time."

Next day the fine weather still held and they went at a good pace. The aches and pains that Cornelia had experienced after the first complete day of walking no longer troubled her as her body became used to the continuing exercise. When they arrived at the camp spot that night Hector suddenly ran off across a field in hot pursuit of something. Their camp was laid out and they were surveying their much depleted food store when suddenly he came back and deposited a dead hare at Cornelia's feet and looked up at her as if to say

"Look what I've brought you. Aren't I clever?"

Paulus picked it up and said "Our supper!"

"How shall we cook it?" asked Cornelia.

"It will go further if we stew it. Luckily we've got Marcus's cooking pot. I'll skin it and clean it and light a fire. You go around and see if anyone will trade a couple of carrots for a couple of apples."

Cornelia did as she was bid and came back with the

requested carrots and some wild thyme and wild garlic, which she had gathered from the roadside. Soon a delicious aroma was rising from the cooking pot. Marcus approached and said "Your dinner smells better than ours."

"Won't you join us?" said Cornelia.

"No, our food is nearly ready. I just brought you a fresh loaf."

"Thank you," said Cornelia and falling on it she broke off a crusty corner and sunk her teeth into it.

"I probably won't see you tomorrow. I probably won't see you until we reassemble in Gaul. I hope you have a good crossing."

Turning to Paulus he said, "Look after her for me."

"As if she were my own," said Paulus, and meant it.

They left a portion of stew in the bottom of the pot for Hector which he devoured at speed. Then Paulus went in search of a stream, although by the time Hector had finished one was hard pushed to see any food on the pot. Paulus must have found a spring or a stream because when he returned it was obvious that he had washed more than the pot and spoons for his hair was damp and he smelt of freshness. Cornelia could not help comparing him with Crassus and had to admit to herself that she was lucky.

As predicted by Marcus they arrived at the coast a day and a half later. They picked a spot behind some rocks and while Cornelia sat and guarded their belongings Paulus went in search of a ship to take them across the water. Cornelia watched as the soldiers boarded the ships and loaded all their horses on board. She caught sight of Marcus a couple of times but he was too far off to see her and was also very busy organising men and equipment. By the end of the day the last of the cavalrymen were embarked and the boats had sailed with the evening tide. A proportion of the camp followers had also departed and there were about twenty or thirty people left sitting around. Paulus returned.

"Did you find something?" asked Cornelia.

"Yes, but not for today. There is a merchant going out tomorrow morning and he is willing to take us across. He can take half a dozen people."

"What time will we go?"

"At dawn."

"How long will the journey take?"

"Most of the day, but it depends on the wind."

Paulus went up into the village and returned with some fishes and a new loaf. He set about lighting a fire and after cleaning the fishes he impaled them on sticks that he wedged between stones so that the fish were over the fire. Cornelia watched this activity admiringly.

"I'm glad you decided to come," she said.

"I didn't have much choice," Paulus replied.

Seated a little way away from them was a lone girl about Cornelia's age. She showed no signs of preparing any sort of meal and Cornelia thought that she was crying.

"Paulus, look at that girl. Do you think we should ask her to share our food? She doesn't seem to have any and she looks very sad."

Though Cornelia had been raised in luxury and never wanted for anything she was not insensitive to the feelings of others.

Paulus looked across at the girl and said "She looks as if she's alone. You go and talk to her, I'll watch the fishes."

Cornelia rose and walked over to the girl.

"Hello," she said. "I couldn't help noticing that you don't seem to have any supper, would you like to share ours?"

The girl looked up at her and as if this kind gesture was the last straw to test her reserve her gentle tears collapsed into desperate sobs. Cornelia, distressed at this display of grief, knelt down beside her and put an arm around her shoulders.

"What's the matter?" she said.

"Nothing really, it's just that I'm so tired and so hungry and Philip has gone."

"Is Philip your man?"

"Yes."

"Well, we'll catch up with the soldiers again in Gaul. Come and sit with us, we have a little wine left. That will put some heart back into you."

"Thank you. You are very kind."

As she scrambled to her feet Cornelia noticed that she was with child. She gathered together her meagre belongings and joined Cornelia and Paulus at their fire.

"Hello," said Paulus. "I'm Paulus."

"And I'm Cornelia. What's your name?"

"I'm Phoebe."

Phoebe sat down and Paulus handed her a fish on a stick.

"Careful, it's hot."

"It smells wonderful."

Cornelia broke the bread and gave a portion to each person. She put half the loaf away for their breakfast. They each ate their fish with their fingers and passed the wineskin around. Cornelia threw bits of her fish to Hector. When they had eaten they all relaxed with their backs against the rocks.

"That is the best fish I have ever eaten. I can't thank you enough," said their new companion.

They settled down to sleep in the lee of the cliffs high up the beach above the high water mark. The sand was silky and warm but by morning they agreed that even though the sand seemed to give under their weight it was not the most comfortable of beds and in the early hours they were aching and cold and they all awoke early. The sun rose in a reddish sky.

"It looks as if it's going to be windy," said Paulus. "Let's hope it's blowing the right way."

Paulus went in search of the merchant with whom the arrangements had been made to tell him that they were now three instead of two while the girls packed up their belongings. They went to relieve themselves in a little niche against the cliffs and were standing waiting when Paulus came back for them.

The ship looked fairly big to Cornelia, like the one's she had seen on the wharves in Londinium though not as wide. They scrambled aboard and the merchant showed them where to stow their bundles and where to sit. They were joined by two other women and a teenage boy and when everyone was well-installed two young men, who were the merchant's sons, pushed the ship offand scrambled aboard. They busied themselves with ropes and sails while their father steered and suddenly the sail filled, the craft leaned slightly and seemed to spring forward. As they drew further and further away from the shore the sea became choppier but the merchant did not seem in the least concerned so Cornelia decided that everything was probably all right. She was enjoying the new sensation. They were all three sitting on the deck just behind the prow with their backs against the side. After about half an hour of riding up and down the waves Phoebe said "I'm sorry but I'm going to be sick."

She knelt up and leaning over the side she was as good as her word. She was very white, almost green and her palms, when Cornelia held her hands, were clammy. Eventually her stomach was empty and she was retching on nothing. Cornelia looked out over the sea and their ship now looked very tiny.

Paulus took the exhausted girl and sat her down on the deck. He wrapped her cloak around her firmly and she eventually fell asleep with her head on his shoulder.

"Do you think she'll be all right?" whispered Cornelia.

"I think so. She's young and looks pretty strong."

Around midday Cornelia took the bread out of her bag and broke a piece off for herself and Paulus. Phoebe stirred but when asked if she would like some she refused.

In spite of the weather the journey was uneventful and it was late one afternoon when they arrived in Gaul. Cornelia was surprised to find that Gaul looked very similar to Britain. She wasn't sure what she thought it would look like but was sure it ought to look foreign.

Phoebe was very wobbly as she came ashore and Paulus had to put a hand under her armpit to steady her.

"I'm sorry I was such a nuisance," she said. "It's the baby. I had stopped having sickness but the sea was a bit too much."

"How much money have we got?" said Cornelia.

"Why?" said Paulus.

"I think, if we can afford it, we should stay at an inn tonight. I'm sure we'll get on better tomorrow if we have a good night's sleep."

"I still have some money," said Phoebe. "Philip gave me enough for the journey."

They went into the fishing village in search of an inn but all they could find was a tavern on the waterfront. Paulus went in and enquired if they could sleep there. He came out and said "There is a room under the tiles that you ladies can share and I can sleep in the stable. Best of all we can have dinner."

"I'm starving." said Phoebe.

"I'm not surprised," said Cornelia, and they all laughed.

A good dinner followed by a night indoors did them all good and the next morning the tavern keeper prepared them a breakfast of bread and warm milk and honey and sold them provisions for the journey. They set off with renewed vigour to catch up with the army and by the following night they spotted the smoke of the campfires not too far off.

They pitched their camp amongst the other camp followers and while Paulus prepared their evening meal Phoebe went off in search of Philip. When she returned she was carrying a loaf of freshly baked bread.

"Ooh, lovely," said Cornelia, as she smelled the warm loaf.

After they had eaten Cornelia made her way to the camp to see Marcus. After a warm embrace he said "I can't come and see you tonight, I'm on duty."

"Will you be free tomorrow night?"

"Yes."

"Can we go for a walk?"

"Don't you think we will all have walked enough?" he smiled.

"I just want to get away from all these people. I want to be on my own with you," and her eyes told him what she felt.

The following evening, as the three travelling companions were setting up their little camp Marcus approached them carrying a cooking pot by a rope handle. As he set it down they could smell the aroma of meat stew.

"Will you join me for dinner?" said Marcus, and from under his cloak he produced a skin of wine. The four of them set to hungrily and as Cornelia wiped the last vestiges of sauce from her bowl with a hunk of bread she thought she had never ever had such a wonderful meal. When everything was finished and the utensils were cleaned and stowed for the morrow Paulus put some more wood on the fire and, rolling himself in his blanket, settled down for the night. Cornelia picked up her own blanket and said,

"We're just going for a stroll. See you later."

As she and Marcus walked off side by side she did not see the look of dismay on Paulus's face. It was as if he knew what was about to take place and wished he were in a position to prevent it. He knew if he tried to stop Cornelia from going off alone with this handsome soldier not only would she put him in his place as a slave but also she would probably be more determined than ever to have her own way. As they walked off he said to her

"Be careful."

"I'll be all right. I'll be with Marcus."

"Yes," he thought, "that's the trouble," but he was powerless to say what he really meant.

"Be careful of wolves, or snakes, or Éthings."

As the two moved out of earshot Phoebe said,

"Try not to be too sad. She'll come back."

Paulus lay down to sleep thinking how unjust life was and how lucky Philip was to have such a homely, sensible girl like

Phoebe and how lucky Marcus was to be free to take any girl he wanted. Why did he have to want Cornelia, and why did she have to want Marcus? He eventually fell into a troubled sleep from which he woke some hours later. The fire was almost dead so he put some more wood on it and saw that Cornelia was still absent.

Cornelia and Marcus strolled together across the fields that bordered the road and looked for somewhere to sit down. The countryside was very open and flat with flocks of sheep grazing on the yellowish grass. Not far off they could see a farmstead, its buildings huddled together and surrounded by a fence. In a small field next to the farm was a small herd of cows. Neither Cornelia not Marcus wanted the company of people at that moment so in silent concord they turned their steps away from the farmstead. There was no woodland in the area but a few yards away they saw a huge standing stone and walked towards it. Marcus removed his cloak and spread it on the ground. They sat close together with their backs against the stone and covered their legs with Cornelia's blanket. Marcus put his arms around her shoulders and she turned her face to his. They kissed long and slowly at first and then their passions took charge and they rolled on the ground inextricably locked together. Marcus made love to her expertly and firmly and Cornelia responded with the energy of her young years. Her pleasure was obvious and she gave herself completely. Eventually they rolled apart and lay on their backs looking up at the sky. By now it was dark and the stars shone down from a sky that was vaster than any she had seen.

"I'm sorry I hurt you. I wanted you so much I forgot you were a virgin"

"That's all right. I wanted you too. Marcus, I love you very much."

Marcus lay quietly for a long time. Cornelia began to feel chilly and pulled the blanket up over them. She snuggled up

to him and when he still said nothing she said "What's up?"
"I don't know what to do with you."
"What do you mean? "
"What do you intend to do when you get to Rome?"
"I don't really know, I hadn't thought."
He lay pensively silent for a while longer then he said "You'll have to go to my mother."
Cornelia really had no fixed idea about what she would do in Rome. In the back of her mind she had taken it for granted that Paulus would protect her and they would live somehow. Living with Marcus's mother was not something she had considered.
"How much do you love me?" asked Marcus.
"I've just shown you how much. Would you like me to show you again?"
He laughed.
"Saucy baggage!"
They laughed, then his voice took on a serious tone.
"I explained to you that I am not allowed to marry while in the army, but we could be pledged to each other. I cannot take you with me when the army send me away but we can spend all my free time together. When we get back to Rome we are going into winter quarters and I shall be able to be at home a great deal. If you are in our house at least I shall know where you are and that you are safe."
"All right," she said, and kissed him again warmly. Their passion was aroused once more and they made love slowly and fondly well into the night

At first light Marcus stirred and woke her gently.
"Come along, we have to move."
They walked across the fields to the direction of the camp and Hector, who had been sleeping between Paulus and the fire, saw her coming and thumped his tail on the ground and gave a little whimper. Paulus put his hand on the dog.
"Stay, boy."

He watched the couple walking hand in hand until they stopped at the parting of their ways. They embraced as they took their leave of each other. Cornelia came back to their little encampment and rolling herself in her blanket she lay down near the dying fire and went straight to sleep with a smile on her lips. Paulus closed his eyes and pretended to be asleep, but he felt as if he had a large stone in the middle of his chest.

Chapter Four

Cornelia saw very little of Marcus over the next days as he was very busy negotiating with local farmers for feed for the horses. As they travelled further away from the coast the countryside began to change. Instead of the flat lands of sandy soil they started to encounter gently rolling hills and the fields and farmsteads were surrounded by expanses of forest. The soil was darker and there were more fields of crops. It reminded Cornelia of home. She had begun lately to think about home and wondered what everyone was doing. She was having what she thought of as a great adventure and it never entered her head that her family might be missing her or be worried about her. She did, however, have a niggling thought that if she went home she would probably be thoroughly punished by her father. But when she thought of Crassus with his watery eyes and wet lips she pushed any doubts she might have out of her mind.

"I had to leave," she thought to herself. "I couldn't possibly marry Crassus; they shouldn't have tried to make me."

This way she told herself that she had done nothing wrong in absconding; she did not consider the fact that she had not actually been forced to marry Crassus. The proposed marriage absolved her from any wrongdoing in her eyes.

As the days passed Paulus became more withdrawn. Cornelia scarcely noticed. Paulus always spoke to her politely but they never had their usual long discussions or exchanged friendly banter. Phoebe saw what was happening and felt sorry for Paulus; after all, though he was a slave he had feelings like any other man. She was powerless to do anything but made an extra effort to speak kindly to Paulus and she took to chatting with him as they walked.

One evening, when they had stopped to camp for the night, Cornelia wandered into the woods bordering the road. She went to search for mushrooms or anything else the forest might afford to supplement their evening meal. She came to a small clearing and spotted a patch of mushrooms in the leaf mould. She was about to go forward to pick them when she heard a rustle in the undergrowth. She kept very still, her heart beating fast. She hoped it was not a wolf, though she knew that wolves only tried to attack people during very cold weather when their normal prey was scarce. Suddenly a sow came blundering out of the undergrowth and, ignoring Cornelia, walked across to the other side of the clearing into the bushes. She was followed by a litter of piglets hurrying after their source of food. Their backs were dappled like the sunlight coming through the leaves and their little tail curled up behind them. The last piglet, obviously the runt, was smaller than the rest of the litter and he had to run faster on his little legs to keep up. He squealed in an agitated manner as if to say "Wait for me, wait for me".

Cornelia laughed and her heartbeat returned to normal, but not for long. She stepped into the centre of the clearing and was about to start gathering the mushrooms when she heard something big crashing about in the undergrowth in front of her. She looked up and froze. In front of her stood a wild boar. Its tusks were larger than any she had seen and its little piggy eyes were looking at her. The beast snorted and prepared to charge this interloper in his domain. Cornelia felt as if her insides had turned to water and she found herself frozen to the spot with fear. The boar gathered itself together and charged. Just when she thought her moment was surely come the boar dropped like a rock a few feet from her. In one of its eyes a spear still quivered. She looked round and saw Paulus behind her. She ran to him and threw herself into the safety of his arms then as the relief of the moment flooded her body she dissolved into tears. Paulus held her tightly and gently stroked her hair.

"It's all right, it's all over now."

They both looked at the boar, which lay motionless before them.

"You saved my life."

He looked at her fondly then gently putting her from him he said, "I promised your father I would make sure no harm came to you."

"Thank you Paulus," she said and the gratitude in her eyes was very real.

"Well," said Paulus, "it looks as if we will be eating well for some days to come."

"What are we going to do? It looks too big for us to manage on our own."

"You stay here and I'll go and get some help."

After a short while Paulus returned with two soldiers who whistled in surprise at the size of the beast he had killed. They removed the spear from the dead animal and tied it together with their own spears. Then they tied the feet together, front and back and threaded the bundle of spears through the legs. Paulus and one of the soldiers heaved the animal up and placing the spears on their shoulders they made their way back to camp. The other soldier and Cornelia walked behind. They entered the Roman camp like a triumphal procession and took their prize to the cook.

The cook was impressed but pointed out that if he were to roast the boar whole it would take most of the night before it was cooked. Paulus volunteered to do his share of stoking the fire and a group of soldiers was designated to keep the fire supplied with fuel and take a turn at watching and turning the meat.

Cornelia went in search of Phoebe to tell her of her adventure and soon the air carried a wonderful aroma of roasting pork. Phoebe was tending their cooking pot over a fire. It contained nothing but an assortment of vegetables. She threw in a few sprigs of wild thyme and the two young women dined hungrily.

"I'll save some for Paulus," said Phoebe and putting the cooking pot to one side she covered it with the piece if wood they used to cut their vegetable on.

Sometime before midnight Paulus returned bearing succulent portions of roast pork. Phoebe said "We saved you some vegetables."

"Thank you," said Paulus and there was a kindly smile in his eyes as he spoke. Cornelia felt a strange little stab of jealousy at the exchange. Paulus was her slave, not Phoebe's, but Phoebe treated him as an equal. Cornelia could not really find anything firm about which she could reprimand him. Paulus always spoke to her very politely and treated her as a lady, but she remembered the friendly banter they had exchanged as children, even into their teens, and wondered when this had stopped. She studied him as they ate their meat and remembered the overwhelming feeling of security she had felt in his arms when he had killed the boar. He had probably saved her life. But then as a slave this is no more that he was supposed to do. She went to sleep that night with strange thoughts in her head. She wished they could arrive in Rome and she could be established as Marcus's betrothed. Everything would be fine then.

Next morning, as they were packing up their small camp Marcus came to them carrying a sack tied at the neck. It contained a generous portion of the now cooked boar. They would have enough to eat for the next few days.

"Congratulations," he said to Paulus as he handed over the sack, "that was a jolly good shot. I've also brought you these as a souvenir," and handed him the two tusks.

"Thank you," said Paulus and put the tusks into his baggage roll.

The cavalry set off once more with its straggling band of followers in tow. Their route took them along good metalled roads and each time they approached a small town or village the road was often lined with small shops where if one had money one could purchase various items of food and other necessary supplies. Whenever they approached a town where the soldiers habitually camped there were even taverns and small inns.

To Cornelia it felt as if they had been walking for months. In fact it was little over a month when they found themselves approaching what was obviously a large and important town. They camped for the night outside the town and once supper was over and they were settling down for the night Marcus and Philip suddenly appeared. Cornelia rose as if to join Marcus but he stopped her.

"No, don't get up," he said. "I want to talk to all of you. Tomorrow we will come to the parting of the ways. This town is Lugudunum, the capital of this part of Gaul. From here we are taking the road to Geneva and are entering Rome over the Alps. It will be much colder there and the road is harder. I think you should continue south to the coast. There is a very good and easy road to Massilia. This is a very busy port where you will be able to get a passage on a ship to Ostia and then up the river to Rome."

"Why can't you come with us?" asked Cornelia.

"Because we have been ordered to march. Don't worry, we'll all arrive eventually. When you arrive in Rome find your way to the Quirinal and ask anyone to direct you to the house of Livia. Here is a letter to give to her in case you arrive first."

Cornelia looked dismayed at the thought of continuing her journey separately from Marcus.

"Can't I come with you? I don't mind if it's cold."

Here Philip intervened and said,

"I would be very grateful if you would go via Massilia and take care of Phoebe for me. She would find the mountain roads too hard in her condition."

The four of them were looking at Cornelia silently. She looked at Phoebe with her big belly and at Paulus with his dependable face and then turned her sad eyes on Marcus.

"All right, I suppose it's best to do as you say."

Philip and Phoebe both gave her a grateful smile and Phoebe hugged her. Marcus gave Paulus a handful of coins.

"This should pay for the ship with a little extra for the rest of your journey. I put my trust in you."

"Your trust will not be betrayed," said Paulus, and he put the coins into the pouch attached to his girdle.

"We have to get back to camp now," said Marcus. "I'll see you in Rome."

Cornelia clung to him as he made his farewell. He kissed her fondly then firmly disentangled her arms and set her a little apart.

"Farewell, may the gods protect you."

Philip hugged Phoebe and said,

"Don't worry, Cornelia and Paulus will protect you until we meet again."

Next morning Cornelia awake to the sounds of the army pulling out. She jumped out of her blanket and ran to the camp. She was in time to see the soldiers marching away in neat formation and she could see Marcus near the front sitting straight on his horse. She watched until they disappeared from view and slowly walked back to her travelling companions. They broke their fast on some bread they had saved from the previous day and drank some cool water. Then, having packed up their belongings they set off towards the city.

The morning was bright and sunny but the weather did not reflect the mood of the travellers. Cornelia was sad at leaving Marcus and silently prayed that all would go well for both of them till they were reunited. Phoebe, also, was anxious but she had the added worry of her unborn child. Paulus was a little worried about not having the security of the army travelling with them and realised that as the only man he was now responsible for their little party. They walked in silence for a while but as they approached the city gates and began to see the size and splendour of the capital of Gaul their mood changed to one of awe as they gazed on street after street of impressive buildings and the wealth of statues and arches. The city was constructed where two great rivers met and the whole town was abuzz with people of every race and colour. They eventually arrived at what Cornelia deduced must be the main forum. In the streets running off from the forum were various markets. Instead of being an agglomeration of stalls of every sort the markets seemed to be grouped according to their wares. There was a street that sold fish, another which sold meat and so on. Around the main square there were shops with a covered arcade running along in front of them and the articles on sale were varied and for the most part luxurious. Cornelia wanted to look at the shops but Paulus said,

"This area seems very expensive. I think we should try and find a more modest area and see if we can find somewhere to eat that will not cost too much. We have to conserve our money."

They crossed a bridge and eventually found themselves in an area that seemed to be devoted to various workshops. They found a modest tavern where they were able to dine on bowls of hot vegetable soup with great chunks of crusty bread. They drank a pitcher of wine and water. They also purchased a roasted chicken, which they wrapped in a cloth and put in one of their bundles for their next meal. Paulus paid the innkeeper and they went out into the street. Unnoticed they were followed by two men who had been dining at the other side of the room. They had seen Paulus take two coins from the pouch attached to his belt and assumed it contained more money. They thought that Paulus's two companions would not present a problem and that the two of them together could easily take care of Paulus. The street was very quiet as most people were in the inns and taverns taking the midday meal. Suddenly an arm came from behind and encircled Paulus's throat. The man was holding an evil looking knife in his other hand. His companion stood in front of the girls brandishing a similar knife.

"If anyone screams he gets the knife in his ribs," said Paulus's assailant. "Cut off his purse," he said to his companion. His companion turned to do as ordered. The second his back was turned Cornelia lifted her foot and kicked him as hard as she could between his legs. The man howled and dropped to the ground clutching his testicles. His companion loosened his hold on Paulus who was able to dig his elbow into the man"s middle. The man puffed hard at the blow and released Paulus completely. Hector, who had been growling threateningly, sank his teeth into the man"s ankle. He howled with pain and tried to shake the dog off

"Run," shouted Paulus and grabbing Phoebe's hand to help her along they took to their heels and ran until they found themselves once more in a bustling square. They leaned up against a wall, panting hard. The girls were visibly shaken. Once they had their breath back Cornelia said,

"That was terrible. How can anyone be so wicked? Do you think they really would have killed us?"

"I think they might have done," said Paulus, then turning to Phoebe he said "Are you all right?"

"Yes, I think so; I'd just like to sit down for a minute."

In the square there was a fountain and two or three women were filling water jars. Paulus led her to the fountain and she sat on the edge of the basin.

"Drink some water," said Paulus.

She cupped her hands under the spout and drank.

"Are you all right dear?" asked a friendly matron.

"Yes thank you, I'm quite recovered."

"What happened?"

"Some men tried to rob us, but we managed to get away."

"Lucky your husband is a big strong lad," said the dame. "How much longer have you got to go?" she asked, indicating Phoebe's swollen belly.

"About another month I think," she replied. She considered explaining that Paulus was not her husband but decided not to bother, it was too complicated to explain to a stranger.

Cornelia looked at Paulus with new eyes. She found it strange that anyone should think he was Phoebe's husband. He was her slave. She was about to offer this information to the dame when Paulus spoke before she did.

"Can you please direct us; we are not sure which way we should go?"

"Where do you want to get to?"

"We're travelling to the coast, to Massilia."

"Ye gods, that's a long way. You need to go south. Take that road there and when you get to the road by the river follow it."

"How long will it take to get to Massilia?"

"I don't rightly know, more than a week."

"Oh that's all right. We've already walked from Britain."

"Ye gods," exclaimed the woman again, "I thought you sounded as if you weren't from these parts."

"Thank you lady," said Paulus.

"Very welcome I'm sure. Good luck on your journey, and good luck with the baby," she said to Phoebe. Paulus lifted her water jar onto her shoulder for her and they went their separate ways.

"I think we should get out of the town and get on our way immediately. We can cover a fair distance before dark."

They set off in the direction indicated and came to the river. They turned left and followed the river until they had left the town behind them. By nightfall they were in open country. Away from the riverbank there were woods and they decided to make their camp amongst the trees. They decided not to light a fire and they shared the cold roast chicken. Cornelia gave Hector a large lump of meat, which disappeared in seconds. Once the evening repast was over they wrapped themselves in their blankets and settled down to sleep. Hector, realising no more food was forthcoming, lay down beside his mistress and soon they all slept.

Next day they arrived at a small town. After their experience in Lugdunum they were wary of entering it but after a discussion they decided they would go in to purchase supplies and continue their journey immediately. They thought if they kept to busy areas and kept their possessions close with their money out of sight they should be safe. They went to the market and bought fruit and vegetables, some cheese and two large loaves of bread. They bought some dried meat which would keep and some sausages. They were just about to leave when they saw another stall and bought a piece of fresh meat for that day and filled their water gourds from the fountain in the square. They shared the carrying of their provisions amongst them and set off once more on their journey.

The dame who had told them that Massilia was about a week's journey away had obviously never walked from her home to the coast. After more than ten days they had still not achieved their destination, but there were more travellers on the road and they struck up a conversation with a small family, a man and his wife and a little girl of about seven, who were walking in the same direction.

"Where are you heading?" said the man to Paulus.

"Massilia, how far is it?"

"Not far, we should be there by tomorrow."

"Have you come far?" asked Paulus.

"From Alba, do you know it?"

"No, we've come from Britain."

The man and his wife looked at them in admiration. The wife chatted to Phoebe and asked her when her baby would come and why they were going to Massilia. The little girl walked with her hand on Hector's head and stroked him as she walked. Hector turned his head and licked her hand and she laughed with delight. That night they all camped together and shared their food. Cornelia felt happier in a larger group; she felt there was safety in numbers.

Next morning the sunshine that had been following them for days had disappeared and the sky was grey and forbidding. By midday they felt the first drops of rain and by mid afternoon they were all thoroughly soaked to the skin. The rain eased at the end of the day and the sunset lit up the remaining clouds with rosy tints. Suddenly, as the air cleared they could see the buildings of a town in the distance.

"There you are," said the man, "that's Massilia."

Everyone was elated by the sight and a new spring came into their previously flagging steps. Except for Phoebe. She was walking more and more slowly and when asked by the wife if she was all right she answered.

"Yes, I'm well thank you, but my back aches."

"We're going to push on and try to get to town as soon as possible. My wife's family is expecting us."

"I should let your friend have a little rest. Good luck with the rest of your journey."

The father hoisted his little daughter onto his shoulders and the little family set off towards the town.

"Do you want a rest?" asked Cornelia of Phoebe.

"No, I'll carry on, but not so fast. That man had very long legs."

Cornelia took three apples out of her pack and gave one each to Phoebe and Paulus and munched on the third one. They walked on slowly but suddenly Phoebe let out a groan of pain and clutching her belly she dropped to her knees in the roadway.

Cornelia stopped at her friend"s side and said "What's the matter?"

After a while Phoebe relaxed and sat back on her heels. She looked up at the faces of her two travelling companions and said,

"I'm sorry, but I think my baby's coming."

Paulus looked around at the surrounding countryside. At the far side of a field he spotted a small building that he took to be some sort of shelter.

"Do you think you can make it to that hut?" he asked.

"I think so," Phoebe replied but before they had reached it she stopped and groaned once more. Paulus carefully picked her up and carried her the last few yards.

The hut seemed to be a shepherd's shelter. It had three stone walls and a roof of brushwood thatch. The floor was covered in a layer of dry straw with lumps of sheep's wool scattered about.

"Spread a blanket on the ground," said Paulus and he lay her down carefully on it.

"Don't worry," said Cornelia, "we'll look after you."

"You stay with her while I go and find some water before it gets too dark," said Paulus, and he set off across the field carrying the cooking pot. He came back carrying the pot, which he had filled from a stream not far off and an armful of sticks. He quickly got a fire going and after he had filled the water gourd he set the pot on the fire.

"When did your pains start?" he said to Phoebe.

"This morning, but I didn't say anything because I didn't want to hold us up. I thought I'd be all right."

Cornelia took a rag and dipped it into the water and wiped Phoebe's face and dry lips.

"Thank you," she said gratefully; then suddenly she shouted

"I want to push," after which she didn't speak to them; she was too busy trying to bring her child into the world. After what seemed like a long time to Cornelia, Phoebe suddenly pulled up her robe and clutched her knees. By the light of the fire Paulus and Cornelia could see the top of the baby's head. A couple more grunts and suddenly the baby slid into the world in a rush of warm water. Phoebe heaved a deep sigh of relief and Paulus lay the baby on its mother's belly.

"Give me your hair ribbon," he ordered Cornelia.

Taking his knife from his belt he cut the ribbon in two then tied each piece on the umbilical cord. He cut through the cord between the ribbons and Cornelia moved the baby up to its mother's nipple. Phoebe put her arms around her son and smiled as he nuzzled her breast then finding the nipple started to suck. Cornelia's face was wet with tears.

"He's beautiful," she said in awe, and she smiled through her tears.

The after-birth came shortly afterwards and Paulus said,

"You help Phoebe to get cleaned up while I go outside and bury this. We don't want to encourage wild animals to come sniffing around."

Cornelia wet a rag in warm water and cleaned Phoebe and wiped the smears of blood from the baby. She opened Phoebe's bundle and took out some clean rags. She wrapped a rag firmly round the baby then laid him on the blanket while she saw to his mother. She took another rag and folded it diagonally over and over. She took a length of soft cord which she tied round Phoebe's middle and fixed the folded rag to it back and front to soak up the blood. She helped Phoebe straighten her clothes and handing the baby back to her she wrapped mother and baby in Phoebe's cloak.

"Thank you," said Phoebe. "I'm so glad you were here."

Hector, who had lain silently guarding the opening of their little shelter during all the activity now ventured slowly inside and went to inspect mother and baby. Then he licked Phoebe's hand, as if to say "I'm glad you're all right again". Phoebe laughed.

Paulus returned.

"Are you all right?" he asked.

"Yes, thank you," said Phoebe. "I'm very thirsty."

Cornelia lifted the water bottle to her lips and she drank deeply, then lying back on the blanket she said,

"I'm very tired," and her eyes shut.

Cornelia looked at Paulus with a new respect and said,

"How did you know what to do?"

"From helping with the animals."

"But you don't tie ribbons on them and cut the cord."

He smiled.

"No, but when a mother cat has kittens she bites through the cord with her teeth. I didn't fancy doing that so I used my knife. I know midwives tie the cord with string so I just did the same."

"You were wonderful," and she smiled gently at him. His

heart felt very full. He returned her gaze silently for a while then broke the spell by saying,

"I'm starving."

Cornelia was suddenly aware of her empty stomach.

"What shall we do?"

"Well, the water's hot. I'll get some more wood for the fire and you cut up what vegetables we've got left and we'll make a soup. There's a little bit of dried meat that will flavour it and half a loaf of bread. That should do till tomorrow."

They saved a piece of bread and some soup for Phoebe and offered Hector a piece of bread soaked in soup. He wolfed this down in a single gulp and looked at Cornelia hopefully. When he realised that there was no more food available he slunk off across the field to hunt for his own supper.

Next morning they were woken by the sound of the baby crying. The fire had gone out and it was chilly. Phoebe said

"I'm starving," and she breakfasted gladly on bread soaked in the cold soup as she fed her baby.

"I think we should get to town as soon as we can," said Paulus.

They gathered their belongings together and Paulus shouldered Phoebe's bundle as well as his own and the little party set off towards the road.

Chapter Five

"We'll wait here for a while," said Paulus.

Cornelia wondered what they were waiting for but her new feeling of respect for Paulus made her obey him without question. Eventually an ox cart came into view driven by a man who, judging from the dusting of flour in his hair and on his clothes, was obviously a miller. His cart was only half full with sacks of flour. Paulus waved him to stop and said,

"I take it you're going to town?"

"I am."

"Please would you let this lady ride on your cart? She gave birth unexpectedly last night before we could get to town and it is rather far for her to walk."

"Welcome," said the miller, and to Phoebe he said, "Boy or girl?"

"Boy," she replied, proudly.

"May the gods bless you both. Is he your first?"

"Yes."

"Lucky you, I've got five daughters."

Cornelia held the baby while Paulus helped Phoebe up onto the cart. They made her comfortable by surrounding her with their bedrolls and bundles and Cornelia put her son in her arms. The miller spoke to his oxen and with Cornelia and Paulus walking beside the cart the little procession made its way into Massilia.

The miller was a chatty fellow and kept up a stream of remarks and information as they trundled along.

"What are you going to Massilia for?" he asked. "You don't sound as if you come from around here."

"We're on our way to Rome," said Cornelia proudly.

"We won't be staying in town long, just until we find a ship," added Paulus.

"We might have to stay a day or two," said Cornelia.

"Well, now there's a stroke of luck, the gods must be smiling on you. I am delivering some of this flour to my wife's brother. He keeps a tavern down by the port. He'll probably be able to give you a room and he knows all the comings and goings in the port. His wife had another little one about a month ago, his third son.

The cart started to descend a hill. The town stretched below and the morning sun was lighting up the sea, which was a sheet of silver dancing wavelets dotted with craft of all sizes. Cornelia was entranced by the view.

As they descended the hill the miller pushed a lever at his side, which applied a brake in the form of a block of wood that pressed against a wheel. Paulus walked at the head of the oxen and restrained them, encouraging them to slow the descent. They arrived at the bottom of the hill and the miller turned his team into a side street and stopped them at the rear of a building.

"Thanks for your help," he said to Paulus, "you obviously know how to handle animals."

"We live on a farm back home," he said as explanation.

"Can you open that gate?" he asked, and Paulus, doing as he was bid swung open a large gate into a yard. The miller manoeuvred his oxen skilfully into the yard.

"You've done that before," said Paulus.

The miller jumped down from his cart and going to an open door he called out "Ho! Mario, come and see what I've brought you".

A swarthy man with bowlegs came out into the yard wiping his hands on a sacking apron. His face creased into a grin and the two men greeted each other with slaps on the back.

"Got my flour I see, and what else have you here?"

"Customers for you. They"re on their way to Rome and need a bed till they find a boat. This young lady's just had her first son," and he indicated Phoebe and her precious bundle. The innkeeper came over and peered at the tiny wrinkled face. The baby seemed to stare at him.

"My, he's got more wrinkles than me," he said. "Come in, come in. I'll call my wife."

He put his head in the doorway and called

"Mimi."

His wife came to the door. She was older than Cornelia but was still young enough to be attractive. Her face was smooth and golden from the sun and her hair was abundantly rich and shiny, the colour of polished oak. She was pleasantly plump and it was obvious from her large breasts that she was a nursing mother.

"These people need beds," said her husband.

Mimi came to the back of the cart and looked at Phoebe's baby. She smiled. "Boy or girl?" she asked.

"It's a boy," replied the proud mother.

"Come inside. Here, let me help you."

Phoebe handed the baby to her and climbed down from the cart. She grabbed her baggage roll and the two women went into the house. Paulus was standing by the men and when the miller went to unload the flour Paulus said, "I'll do that. Where do you want it?"

"Take it through to the kitchen, there's a flour bin."

Cornelia stood not knowing what to do. Hector had found a shady corner and was lying down on the cool flagstones of the yard. Everybody seemed to have forgotten about Cornelia. She went into the kitchen feeling somewhat neglected. The two mothers were ensconced on a settle feeding their babies and chatting companionably together. They looked up as Cornelia came in.

"Come in my dear," said Mimi. "As soon as this greedy chap has had his fill I'll get you some food. You must be hungry."

"I need a dish to give some water to Hector," she said.

"There's a trough in the yard. Ask Mario to draw a pail of water from the well."

She went out into the yard once more. The flour sacks for the inn were unloaded and the tail of the cart was closed.

Their bundles were lying on the ground against the house wall. Mario was drawing water from the well to fill the trough for the oxen to drink and Hector was waiting expectantly by the trough with his pink tongue hanging out. Cornelia felt as if she were almost invisible. She cast around for something to do and saw the latrine in the far corner of the yard. She walked over there and relieved herself. When she came out the yard was empty. She returned to the kitchen. The men had occupied the settle and Mimi and Phoebe were engaged in preparing a meal. A curly headed toddler was sitting on Mario's knee and a slightly larger but almost identical little boy was squeezed between his father and his uncle. The two babies were sleeping top to toe in a wooden cradle in a dark corner of the room.

Cornelia looked around for somewhere to sit. The only spot she could find was the window ledge. She perched herself on it and waited. She was feeling strange, as if she were invisible to everyone in the room. At home she had sometimes been chastised by her parents. She had been teased by her brother and even had heated arguments with Paulus when they were children. But she had never been ignored. She was not sure how to make her presence felt. Then Mario addressed the three of them.

"We've only got one spare room," he said. "Do you think you can all squeeze in? It will probably only be for one or maybe two nights. There's a ship loading olive oil that is bound for Ostia. He might sail tomorrow," and turning to Paulus he said, "I'm sure you and your wife won't mind being a bit squashed for a night."

Paulus opened his mouth to speak but before he could utter Cornelia said, in a haughty tone,

"Paulus is not my husband, he's my slave."

A silence fell.

"Sorry, we didn't know," said Mimi.

"That's all right," said Paulus. "The girls can have the room. I shall be fine here or even in the outhouse."

The sleeping arrangements settled, Mimi busied herself with food. She placed a jug of wine on the table and a large platter full of chunks of crusty bread. For each person she ladled out a generous portion from a large pot that was simmering over a brazier. It was a stew made of various types of fish and richly flavoured with herbs. It was a flavour entirely new to the three Britons but after the first tentative spoonful they declared it delicious and fell to with gusto. The food gave them new energy and restored Cornelia's usual good humour. When she still had some stew in her dish she soaked some bread in it and picking up her dish made as if to go to the yard. Mimi looked at her questioningly and Cornelia said, "It's for Hector."

"Don't give him your food," said Mimi, "I'll get him something when we've finished. You finish you food first," she said smiling.

"Thank you," said Cornelia.

Once everyone had had his fill of stew a large platter of fruit appeared. There were purple grapes, peaches with a downy bloom and plump blushing apricots. Cornelia regaled herself and said to Mimi "That was wonderful, I've had grapes before but I've never seen them so large or tasted anything so delicious, and the fish stew was excellent."

"They do say hunger makes the best sauce, and I think you were all very hungry."

"We were running out of food by the time we got here," said Paulus.

"I have to confess that since the baby was born I've thought a great deal about food," said Phoebe.

Mimi laughed. "I know what you mean," she said.

Mimi prepared a bowl of food for Hector and took it out to the yard, closely followed by her two sons. Hector stood up and stretching his neck he sniffed expectantly. When he realised that he was to be the recipient of the dish his tail wagged and he attacked the food voraciously. The two boys squatted down on their haunches and watched the rapidity with which the plate was cleaned. Mimi came back in and said,

"I'll show you to your room and once you've sorted yourselves out I'm sure you've got some things that need washing, especially after the birth. Bring everything into the yard and we'll put it to soak."

By the time Cornelia and Phoebe awoke next morning Paulus had been long gone. Mario had taken him down to the water front to find the captain of the boat that was loading for Ostia. The two men returned to the inn before midday with the news that all was arranged. The journey would take between two and three days depending on the wind and a price for the journey had been agreed that would include one meal a day. They were to leave that afternoon. Cornelia was excited at the prospect that she would reach her destination in a matter of a few days but although Phoebe was also undoubtedly glad that she would soon be safe in Philip's home she was apprehensive about the journey, especially after the memory of their last sea voyage. Mimi looked at the young mother's anxious face.

"Don't worry," she said, "you'll be fine. We don't normally get storms this month, they come later. You'll be there before you know it," and turning the subject to more practical matters she said, "Your linens are all dry. You go and pack all your things together and I'll prepare you a basket of bread and fruit for the journey. Then we'll have some food before you go."

An hour later saw the trio, Phoebe carrying her baby, wending their way down the hill to the port. Paulus led them towards a merchant ship that was tied up at the quay and called a greeting to the captain. There was a great deal of activity on the deck as the little crew prepared the ship for departure. Paulus motioned Cornelia to cross the gangplank first and Paulus followed behind helping Phoebe who was less sure-footed. A member of the crew, who turned out to be the cook, showed them where to settle themselves and then went back to his duties coiling ropes.

The ship was pushed off from the quayside with long poles and as the sail was hoisted they sailed slowly out of the harbour towards the open sea. As they left the port and drew away from the land Phoebe's apprehension faded and she relaxed visibly. The sea was serene with tiny dancing wavelets and the afternoon sun made it shine like silver. The sail bellied out but the ship remained almost upright as it increased speed.

Once they were well under way the cook went to a place on the small deck behind the mast where a pottery brazier sat. He struck a light with a flint and with the aid of some tarred, teased out bits of rope he kindled a fire in the brazier. Once the charcoal was well alight he set a cooking pot on the stove and then calmly unrolled a blanket and lay himself down on the deck to sleep. Phoebe fed her baby and eventually they too were both asleep.

Cornelia watched with interest as the land receded until it was no more than a dark line in the distance and looking past the stern of the boat she saw the sun getting lower and lower until it seemed to be sitting on the horizon. She wondered idly what would happen to the sun when it eventually went down into the sea and asked herself if it would get wet. With this strange thought on her mind she fell asleep. Hector laid his head on her lap and joined her in the land of dreams.

When they awoke it was almost dark and the cook was doling portions of stew into bowls. He gave a bowl to everyone on board except the man at the helm and the sailor in charge of trimming the sails who would be relieved of their tasks and take their turn later. He poured goblets of wine from an amphora and handed these around along with a hunk of bread. He then fished around in the bottom of the cooking pot and pulled out a knucklebone, which he presented to Hector. Cornelia dipped some of her bread in her gravy and fed it to Hector who wagged his tale in thanks. When the meal was finished it was completely dark. The sky was studded with stars and all around them the sea was dark.

The cook, when he came to collect the dishes, indicated to them a latrine built over the side of the deck where they could relieve themselves and Cornelia took Hector with her and persuaded him to perform the necessary function. Phoebe whispered something to Paulus and he went to speak to the cook. He came back with a pail of water that he had drawn from overboard and Phoebe put all the linens she had used that day from the baby and herself. Everyone lay down to sleep wrapped in their blankets and cloaks and they all drifted off to slumber to the gentle sounds of the waves swishing along the boat's sides and the creaking of the rigging while one of the sailors softly sang a song in a language they could not understand.

Their journey was uneventful and Phoebe was surprised to find it really restful. By the third day Cornelia was restless. Her young, energetic body was beginning to rebel against the forced inactivity and it was with great joy that they sighted land, which the captain told them was their destination. The land was just a smudge on the horizon but as the day progressed the smudge grew and grew until they could see trees and buildings. The afternoon was well advanced when they finally dropped their sail and the boat nudged its way to the quayside. Willing hands on shore grabbed the ropes that were thrown to them and two sailors took the gangplank and shot it out from the ship's side till it rested on the quay. Paulus shouldered his bundle as well as those of his two companions and Cornelia carried the basket. They made their farewells to the captain and his crew and thanked them then one by one made their way down the gangplank onto Imperial soil.

Hector immediately lifted his leg and peed a long pee against a bollard. They all laughed.

"He's pouring a libation to show his gratitude," said Cornelia. They made their way along the quay past rows of warehouses bustling with activity towards the town of Ostia.

"Where are we going?" asked Cornelia.

"Philip explained to me where his mother lives but he did not know which harbour we might land in so I'm not too sure. But he said that most people know her house."

"Well, let's ask someone," said Cornelia.

Paulus said, "What's her name?"

"Hermione," answered Phoebe.

Paulus approached a man who was directing operations loading goods onto a barge.

"Hermione's? Yes, surely, walk along that street there and at the end turn left and you'll see it along on the right. It has a blue door and tables outside."

They followed his directions and soon found what the building that were seeking. One or two of the tables on the pavement outside were occupied by sailors drinking wine and at one table a family with three children were tucking in to what smelled like a delicious meal. A young woman was filling the sailors' goblets from a ewer. Phoebe went up to her and waited until she had completed her task then,

"Hello, are you Helena or Penelope?" she asked her.

The girl leaned the ewer on her hip and said,

"I'm Helena. Can I help you?"

"I'm Phoebe. I'm looking for Hermione."

"Phoebe, how wonderful! Come in, mother's inside."

They followed Philip's sister into the tavern.

Hermione was standing behind a serving counter ladling food onto platters.

"Mother, this is Phoebe," said Helena.

Hermione looked up and gazed intently at Phoebe. She obviously liked what she saw because she smiled and came into the centre of the room.

"How lovely to see you," she said. "Philip wrote that you were coming but did not know exactly when."

"Have you seen him?" Phoebe asked.

"No, but we expect him on leave any day quite soon." She looked at the little bundle in Phoebe's arms. "We didn't expect the baby to be born yet," and as she looked enquiringly at

Cornelia and Paulus she added, "and we thought you would be alone."

"These are my friends, Cornelia and Paulus. They are on their way to Rome. The baby was born a little sooner that I thought."

Hermione and her two daughters looked with interest at the little puckered face.

"Is it a boy or a girl?" asked Hermione.

"A boy," answered Phoebe.

"Doesn't he look like Philip?" said Helena.

"He looks a bit like father did," said Penelope.

"Well Philip looked like father," said Helena.

"What's his name?" asked Hermione.

"I haven't really given him a proper name yet, I was waiting for Philip to decide, but I"d like to call him after the midwife who helped me give birth for one of his names."

"What was she called?"

"It wasn't a she, it was Paulus. It happened suddenly one night in a field. I'm calling him Paulinus"

"In a field! You poor thing," said Hermione, and she gently took her grandson from Phoebe's arms and gazed at his little face.

"He's lovely. Penelope, take Phoebe up to Philip's room. Helena, see that hot water is taken up for her to wash."

She handed the baby back and added, "and then come down to eat."

She looked at Paulus with a certain respect and said "Thank you for taking care of them."

Once more Cornelia felt as if she were living on the fringe of events but did not know how to enter into the conversation. Paulus was her slave. They were there because she, Cornelia, had decided to come. If it were not for her they would never have been here. As she was standing wondering what to say the situation was saved by Hector who moved over to the serving counter and lifting his muzzle sniffed the food that was sitting on the platters.

"Hector! Come here," said Cornelia firmly. Hector dropped his tail and slunk over to Cornelia's side.

"What an obedient dog," Hermione remarked. "You must all be hungry. There's a washhouse in the yard with a well. Go and get some of the dust of your journey off and then come and eat," and she took a platter of food and put it down on the paving stones of the yard for Hector to eat.

An hour later saw them all sitting under the shade of a vine in front of the tavern with empty platters in front of them. Little Paulinus was fed and in a rosy-cheeked stupor in his grandmother's arms. Cornelia said,

"Can you tell us the best way to get to Rome, and how long will it take?"

"Oh, not long. The best way is to take a barge from here up the river. There are a great many making the journey every day. You'll be able to get one early in the morning. I'll get someone to find you one. In the meantime you can sleep here. The girls can share for one night and you and your husband can have one of their rooms."

Once more Cornelia had to explain the situation. Why did people always take Paulus and her for man and wife?

"Paulus is my slave," she said, in a slightly haughty manner. "I am travelling to Rome to be with my betrothed. He is a cavalry officer. Philip is one of the men travelling with him."

Paulus took a renewed interest in the scraps of food left on his plate and did not look up.

"I do apologise," said Hermione, "We did not know. Never mind, you can have one of the girls" rooms and Paulus can sleep in the kitchen."

Next morning early Cornelia entered the kitchen to find it empty. She went into the yard to the latrine and was greeted by Hector. As she returned to the kitchen she found Hermione pouring milk into a cooking pot.

"Where's Paulus?" she asked.

"Good morning," said Hermione, "I hope you slept well."

Once more Cornelia felt wrong footed. What was the matter with her? Why was she behaving as if she had never been taught her manners? Chastened she made an attempt to put the situation to rights. She apologised for her lapse and assured Hermione that she had slept like a log and was very grateful for her hospitality. Hermione gave her a friendly smile and said

"Paulus has gone down to the riverside quay with one of my regular customers to find a barge that is setting off for Rome this morning. He should be back soon. You go and pack up your things and I'll prepare something to break your fast."

A couple of hours later Cornelia, Paulus and Hector were taking their leave of Phoebe and her newfound family. Phoebe embraced Cornelia fondly and said

"I hope I'll see you again, Rome isn't very far away. I wish you everything good and hope all goes well with Marcus."

Then she put her arms around Paulus and gave him a big friendly hug. "Thank you for everything you did for me and the baby. I wish you luck."

She patted Hector, who licked her hand and gently wagged his tail.

Cornelia remembered her manners and embraced Hermione and her daughters and thanked them for all their help and hospitality and promising to return one day for a visit they waved "good bye" and set off towards the quay.

Chapter Six

The twilight was deepening and lights were twinkling in the houses as Cornelia and Paulus made their way up the Quirinal Hill as Marcus had directed. Near the top Paulus approached a man in the street and asked for directions to the house of Livia and another ten minutes found them knocking on the door of a very large, imposing building. The front of the building that held the door consisted of half a dozen shops that fronted the road. The shutters were either up or being erected for the night and a young lad who was dropping the cross bars into place in front of the nearest shop looked at them inquisitively. They heard the gentle slap of sandaled feet on the other side of the door and a small window in the centre of the door opened and a face asked them their business.

"I am here to see the Lady Livia," said Cornelia. Although her voice was strong and confident her stomach was full of butterflies. The little window was closed abruptly and there was the noise of a bolt sliding then the door opened. A manservant was standing before them and obviously did not know what to make of this couple who came calling on foot asking for his mistress. The man was clearly a slave but the girl was not really dressed for visiting.

"What is your business?" he asked as he invited them into the atrium.

Cornelia was about to answer when a very elegant lady came from a doorway on the far side of the room.

"What is it Solon?"

"A young lady to see you, my lady."

Cornelia stepped forward and handing the lady Marcus's letter said "Your son, Marcus, has sent me to you."

Livia was taller than Cornelia and she carried herself very straight. Her hair had once been ebony coloured but now contained a lot of silver streaks. It was elegantly dressed in curls on top of her head and was held in place by a silver mesh band. Her robe was pale blue and pinned at the shoulders with finely wrought blue enamel brooches. The tassels of a silver cord girdle hung from her waist. She took the letter from Cornelia and unfolded it with white, long-fingered hands that wore two jewelled rings. She recognised her son's handwriting.

"Come into my study," she said. "Your slave can sit here," and she indicated a marble bench against the wall. Cornelia followed her through a door in the far corner of the hall and found herself in a small room furnished with a writing table and chair and a long sofa along one wall. The wall behind the desk was covered in wooden shelves and pigeonholes that were full of rolls of documents tied with fine cord and stacks of parchment.

"Take a seat," said Livia indicating one end of the sofa and she sat herself at the other end while she read the letter. When she had finished she looked up and looked keenly at Cornelia. After what seemed like an age she spoke.

"Well," she said. "Marcus was always one for knowing what he wants and usually getting it. I have to say that you are a very pretty girl. What is your background and how did you get here?"

"My father owns an estate (she thought "estate" sounded better than "farm") in Britannia. He wanted me to marry someone called Crassus but I love Marcus. Crassus makes my flesh creep. So I came to Rome."

"But how did you get here?" she asked again.

"I walked."

"All the way from Britannia!"

"Yes, but I followed the army a lot of the way. Quite a number of people do."

Livia looked at Cornelia with amazed respect for her feat then said,

"If you followed Marcus's unit how did you manage to arrive here before Marcus?"

"After Lugdunum we split up. The army had to go over the mountains but we went directly to the coast and came by ship to Ostia. He should arrive soon."

"Well! You do seem to be a very resourceful young lady. I suppose we'd better find you a little corner somewhere. Welcome to my home," and she embraced Cornelia gently on the cheeks.

This unexpected sign of acceptance took Cornelia by surprise and coming as it did after weeks of travel, hardship and deprivation touched her emotions so much that she dissolved into floods of tears.

"Come come, there's no need to cry, everything will be fine."

She rose and went into the atrium. Cornelia followed, rubbing away her tears with the back of her hand. Livia clapped her hands sharply and the same slave who had opened the door materialised as if from thin air.

"Solon, this is Cornelia. She is my son's friend who will be staying with us. Ask Beata to take her to the yellow room and see that she has all she needs. This is her slave," turning to Paulus she asked "what is your name, slave?"

"Paulus, my lady."

"Take Paulus up to the attic and install him in one of the empty rooms. Show him where everything is and then take him to the kitchens and see that he is fed. The dog can go to the kitchen yard."

"Excuse me," said Cornelia as politely as she could, "but Hector is my dog and he has never been separated from me. At home he slept under my bed."

"Very well. I hope he is well behaved."

"Perfectly. Mother often said his manners were better than mine."

Livia laughed then said,

"When you have washed and changed dinner will be served."

The slave, Beata, took Cornelia's bundle and led the way to her new room. The "little corner" that Livia had promised her was one of the prettiest apartments she had ever seen. The bed was covered with a buttercup yellow silk coverlet and piled with pillows in various shades of yellow. The floor had a simple mosaic and the walls were painted in deep ochre at the bottom and pale blue above with mimosa trees in full bloom depicted all around. As well as the bed there was a wooden chest and against the wall a small table and stool. An alcove in one corner was curtained off with a saffron coloured curtain and it contained a washstand with a bowl, various jugs for water and a chamber pot.

"I'll bring you some water to wash, tomorrow morning you can go to the bathhouse," and she deposited Cornelia's bundle on the bed.

She had no sooner left the room than a voice from the doorway said "Hello, I'm Claudia, Marcus's sister. It's nice to see you," and she smiled warmly as she inspected Cornelia. Claudia resembled her brother in colouring and she had the same chestnut curls but her eyes had a different expression. Whereas Marcus's eyes had the same deep brown sympathetic look of his mother's Claudia's eyes had tawny flecks in the brown and they held a mischievous twinkle.

"Hello. You look like Marcus, but somehow different," said Cornelia.

"I'm glad about that," said Claudia, and the two girls laughed. Claudia went on to add, "They say I look like our father, but I can hardly remember him. Marcus is more like mother." Then looking at Cornelia's meagre bundle she said

"Have you got everything you need? Would you like to borrow a clean robe for dinner? We can get your things washed tomorrow."

"That would be kind," said Cornelia. "My things are a bit scruffy after the journey. Everything here is so beautiful and fresh, I''d forgotten what it's like to be in a proper house."

"You get washed and I'll go and see what I can find, we're about the same size."

By the time she was washed and dressed in a fresh robe

belonging to Claudia, and the slave had arranged her hair for her, Cornelia walked into the dining room feeling like the lady she was about to become. Livia gave her a look of satisfied appraisal and smiling said, "Come and sit by me. I want to hear all about your journey and all about Marcus. He's not the world's best letter writer."

Cornelia told Marcus's mother and sister how she had met Marcus and related various anecdotes concerning their journey from Britannia. By the time the last course was served and Cornelia was eating a plate of purple figs in a sweet sauce her storytelling started to flag. Livia saw Cornelia's eyelids drooping and suggested that she should retire for the night and continue with their conversation next day.

"Yes, I am rather tired; it suddenly seems as if it was a very long journey. I just want to thank you for your very kind hospitality."

"You don't have to thank me," said Livia. "It's the least I can do for my future daughter. Sleep well."

Cornelia kissed the older woman gently on the cheek then embraced Claudia and said, "Thank you for the loan of your robe. Good night."

"Goodnight, sleep well."

Next day when Cornelia awoke the sun was already high in the sky. She rose from her bed and slipped on the robe she had worn the night before and went in search of breakfast. As she entered the atrium she was greeted by Claudia who was sitting at a table and writing on a large scroll.

"Hello sleepyhead, I thought you were never going to wake up. Breakfast was cleared away ages ago, but I'm sure we can find you something."

She clapped her hands and a slave girl brought in a platter of little cakes and a variety of fruits along with a small jug that contained wine and water and placed them on a little side table. In spite of having dined well the previous evening she attacked the food with a good appetite.

"What are you doing?" she asked Claudia.

"I'm bringing the accounts up to date."

"How did you learn how to do that? I can read Greek and can sew. I can just about cope with ordinary domestic accounts but that looks very complicated?

"Not really. It's the same as ordinary domestic accounts only bigger. We have a janitor who looks after collecting rents and logging complaints and requests from our tenants but father always used to take care of everything. He said if you leave all your financial affairs to someone else you could never be sure you are not being cheated. After he died mother used to do it but she decided it would be a good thing if I learned how to do it and it's actually very interesting."

"I don't think I could ever do that," said Cornelia.

"Yes you can. I'll teach you if you like. After all, once Marcus has finished with the army he will take over the running of the property and as his wife you'll have to know what's going on."

Cornelia absorbed this scenario very slowly. She had never thought beyond belonging to Marcus and possibly giving him children. She had never considered the day to day running of life and had not envisaged herself doing anything specific towards it. Her mother was concerned only with the smooth running of the domestic side of life; the business side of things was taken care of by her father and would eventually be run by her brother. She had never thought she would have any part in any of it. She looked at Claudia with interest.

"I suppose you're right, I hadn't thought of it. Show me what to do."

Claudia laughed gently at her enthusiasm.

"Not today," she said, "there'll be plenty of time for that. You should settle in first. How would you like to go for a walk around the city this afternoon?"

"Oh yes please," she replied eagerly, "I'd love that."

"Fine. As soon as the afternoon grows a little cooler we'll take a stroll. We'll take Paulus with us as he needs to learn his way about too. Now let's call Beata and we'll go to the baths, there's just about enough time before the men"s session starts." She rolled up her scroll and placed her pen on the table. The little slave girl came to remove the remains of Cornelia's meal and Claudia told her to summon Beata for their trip to the baths. Beata appeared carrying a basket containing an assortment of towels, oils and various cosmetic implements.

"Shall we take a chair or do you mind walking?"

"I've just walked from Britannia so I think I can manage the baths," said Cornelia, and amid laughter the three set off. Hector, who had been lying on the cool marble floor of the atrium rose as if to accompany them.

"No Hector. Stay!" said Cornelia, and Hector flopped down once more as if glad he did not have to venture out into the heat.

"He really is a very obedient dog," said Claudia.

The baths was the biggest building Cornelia had ever seen. It contained many vast rooms all of which were extremely luxurious in their appointments. It was very noisy and the sounds seemed to be amplified by the height of the roof. Cornelia gazed around spellbound.

"This is enormous!" she said.

"Have you been to a baths before?"

"Oh yes. I've been to the baths in Londinium, but they were not as big as this."

"Don't you have a bath near your home? What about the army camp? Aren't you allowed to use that?"

"Oh we have a bath house at home, but of course it's quite small, and it's only got two rooms."

The two girls undressed and left Beata in charge of their clothes as they made their way through the various rooms. They eventually arrived in the caldarium, a circular room under a domed ceiling. Here they sat in the hot water after having scraped each other with strigils to remove the oil they had applied.

"Will you ever marry?" asked Cornelia.

"I might. But I have to think of mother as well. She needs someone to help her run the flats so I can't really leave her, and Marcus can't be there. I might marry someone who will live with us and take over but mother would rather I married someone who has his own money and his own house."

Cornelia thought about the situation and said

"Well perhaps I could learn to help. As Marcus has to stay in the army for some time I can't go anywhere. You could show me what to do."

"Are you any good at organising slaves?"

"Oh yes. We have a lot of slaves at home, and I'm sure I could cope with the calculations if you showed me"

"We'll see. I think you ought to settle in first. Then we'll wait for Marcus to come home and see what he says."

At that point a matronly woman came through calling that the women must leave the baths in the next hour so the two young women climbed out of the water and after a quick plunge in the cold bath they went back to the changing room to dress. As they arrived home they were called for the main meal of the day after which everyone retired to their bedrooms until the heat of the day had passed. Cornelia was sure she would not sleep but she decided a little rest on her bed would be pleasant after her morning at the baths. She kicked off her sandals and lay down on her bed and late in the afternoon, when Claudia came to her room Cornelia was surprised to realise that she had, in fact, slept for more than two hours and the previously glaring midday sun was now lower in the sky and bathing the world with a much gentler light.

"Ready? asked Claudia.

"Yes," she answered eagerly, "I'll just tidy my hair."

"I've sent someone to fetch Paulus," said Claudia, and indeed Paulus was waiting for them in the atrium, with Hector at his heels.

They stepped out into the dusty street and Cornelia

breathed in the odours of Rome. As they descended the hill towards the Forum the crowds increased and the air was full of the sounds and smells of the busy city. There were scents of charring meat and cooking spices as they passed eating shops, new bread as they passed a baker's, ammonia as they passed the fuller's shop. The fullers collected urine from special receptacles in front of their shops that they used to whiten cloth. There were the smells of fruit as they passed a stall displaying citrus fruits that Cornelia had never seen before as well as peaches and grapes. There was the smell of humanity, some bodies washed and perfumed and some definitely unwashed. Then, as they left Ceasar's Forum and descended the hill the smell of the river reached them before they saw it. The area by the river was abuzz with activity, even at this late hour, and there were a number of people, like them, strolling in the cooler evening air. There were boats tied to the riverside and stalls dotted around selling sausages and sweetmeats and drinks of various colours made from different fruits. Both Cornelia and Paulus gazed about wide-eyed. Claudia pointed out various important buildings, arches, temples, sumptuous houses and shady gardens.

"This is the oldest bridge across the Tiber," she said. "Of course now there are a lot more."

A nursemaid was walking along holding the hand of a little boy of about three. They were accompanied by a black slave. Cornelia had never seen anyone so black before and she was marvelling at the colour of his skin and his incredibly curly hair when there was a sharp scream from the nursemaid followed by a splash. The little boy had slipped her hand and run to the edge of the riverside the better to see a monkey that was climbing about on the rigging of a boat. He had fallen into the water, between the boat and the quay and his nurse was hysterical. The slave stood glued to the spot. Suddenly there was a second, bigger splash and Cornelia realised that Paulus had jumped into the river. He grabbed the floundering child by his tunic and swam with him down stream away from the boat. He found the rungs of a ladder in the embankment and putting the boy over his shoulder he grasped a rung and hauled himself up. He laid the inert form of the child on the quayside and turning him on his face he applied pressure to his back. The boy suddenly spluttered and regurgitated a quantity of Tiber water then started to howl. The nurse by this time was also crying, partly from relief but the slave was still immobile on the spot.

"Where do you live? I'll carry him home for you," said Paulus

"Thank you, thank you. I don't know what would have happened if you had not been there."

"Why didn't your slave save him?"

"He can't swim. He was actually shipwrecked coming from Africa and spent two days clinging to a piece of wood so he's very frightened of water."

Paulus, carrying the child, who had by now stopped crying, walked along by the side of the nurse. They were followed by Claudia and Cornelia who were closely followed by Hector. The black slave took up the rear. They stopped at a large, imposing gate and the nurse rang a bell at the side. The gate was opened by an older man who, on seeing the procession opened both the gate and his mouth wide.

"What happened?" he said.

"The young master fell into the river. This person saved him."

The nurse took the now calm child and hurried away with him. The black slave had disappeared. The doorman looked at Paulus standing dripping gently onto the marble floor and then at his two companions.

"Would you wait here please?" he said, "while I fetch the master."

He rushed away leaving the three of them to gaze in awe at their surroundings. The atrium was the most sumptuous any of them had seen, even Claudia. The mosaics on the floor were fine and beautifully executed and the walls were decorated with vivid colours and paintings depicting hunting scenes. The pictures gleamed with touches of gold and they were framed by pillars of red marble. In the centre of the atrium was a pool with a fountain in its centre.

"This family must be seriously wealthy," said Claudia.

They were all wondering what to do when the door slave came back and addressing Paulus he said "Would you come with me please, the master wishes to see you. Ladies, would you take a seat in this room here," and he indicated a side door.

Paulus followed him through the atrium and into a door at the other end. This was a study, judging from the shelves of papers around the walls and seated behind an impressive writing table there was a man who Paulus placed in his mid thirties. He was wearing a toga and was clean-shaven and well groomed.

"Please sit down young man."

"I"d better not sir, I'm rather wet."

At this the man himself stood and came to the front of the table.

"I hear I owe you a huge debt".

"Not at all, I only fished the boy out of the water."

"You almost certainly saved his life. My young son is very precious to me. I want to show my gratitude," and so saying he took a leather pouch that was on the table and handed it to Paulus. It chinked and was heavy.

"I don't know what to say," said Paulus. "Thank you sir. I did not expect a reward."

"It is I who have to thank you. Now I must go and see my son," and he clapped Paulus on the shoulder as he accompanied him to the door.

"May I return to find out how the little man fares? He drank quite a lot of river water and it does not look the cleanest water I've seen."

"By all means. My slave will see you out," and he left Paulus to go to his son. Paulus fastened the strings of the pouch to his belt and slipped the pouch itself into the pocket at the side of his tunic. He returned to the atrium where the two girls and Hector were waiting.

"What did he want?" asked Cornelia.

"Just to thank me for saving his son," said Paulus.

"I've seen that man before," said Claudia. "I think he's a senator."

"I would like to go home now if you don't mind. I'm very wet. We can come back another day to see how the boy is."

When they arrived home Paulus went up to his garret to change and to put his reward in a safe place. When he opened the pouch in the privacy of his room his eyes opened wide. It was full of coins, as he had suspected, but the coins were all gold. He was looking at a small fortune. He stripped off his wet clothes and donned some dry ones then looked around for a safe spot for his treasure. He decided to secrete it in his mattress. He took out one gold coin which he slipped in his pocket and tucked the rest away. He would tell no one of the extent of his good fortune, but he knew what he was going to use it for. He could at last see his greatest dream realised.

That evening at dinner Claudia told her mother of the day's event.

"The house was magnificent. I've never seen such surroundings except in a temple. We only saw the atrium but that was enough to take your breath away. I think the father is a senator. I'm sure I've seen him before, in a procession."

A couple of days later all three of them went once more to the house and when the doorman opened the door it was Cornelia who spoke.

"Good day. We have come to enquire after the health of the son of the house. My slave pulled him out of the river two days ago."

"Come in, my ladies, come in," and he opened the door wide.

As they stood in the atrium a little figure suddenly came running into the room on his little fat legs and with a whoop leapt onto Paulus. His nursemaid came running after him admonishing him to remember his manners.

"You pulled me out of the river," said the child.

"And what must you say?" said the nurse.

"Thank you for saving my life," he recited.

Paulus placed the child on the floor and crouching down so that their faces were level Paulus said, "That's quite all right. But promise me you'll never let go of your nurse's hand again when you're by the water."

"I promise."

"He does not seem to have suffered any ill effects from his dunking," said Claudia.

"No, he's fine," replied the nurse, and looking at Paulus she said,

"I can't thank you enough for what you did."

"Don't mention it, anyone would have done the same," he replied with a smile.

Cornelia took command of the situation by saying "I'm glad my slave could be of use to you. We must continue with our walk now. We just wanted to be sure the little fellow was all right."

As they left the house and descended the hill Claudia was left with the impression that Cornelia had been somehow put out by the attention that Paulus had received. If it were not for the fact that he was a slave she might have suspected Cornelia of being jealous, or perhaps she was just accustomed to being the centre of attention. When they arrived home all thoughts of Cornelia's being jealous of Paulus vanished because there, standing in the atrium was Marcus. Cornelia gave a cry of delight and ran to his arms. He embraced her with warmth then releasing her, but keeping hold of her hand, he turned to greet his sister. As he kissed her cheeks she said,

"How long have you been here?"

"An hour at least, and what do I find when tired and weary after weeks of marching right across the empire, my own sister and my betrothed out visiting the high and the mighty."

The girls laughed and Claudia said,

"It's nice to have you home."

"How long have you got?" asked Cornelia.

"I've just arrived and she's already asking me when I'm leaving. Are you telling me something? Perhaps you're tired of me already"

"Oh Marcus, I'm so glad to see you," she said and the two of them hugged each other once more.

Later, over dinner, Marcus told them about his journey over the Alps and Cornelia related all that had happened to her after they had parted company. She told him about the men who had tried to rob them and how Hector had bitten the man"s ankle. She told him about Phoebe's baby and about their boat trip from Massilia. Twilight had deepened into dusk and the slaves had lit the lamps by the time all their storytelling was done. The time to retire for the night arrived and Cornelia did not want to be the first to leave the table. She desperately wanted to spend some time alone with Marcus but did not see how this could be contrived without offending her hostess and in spite of the fact that she and Marcus had slept together on their journey she did not want his mother to think her any other than correctly brought up. Livia herself solved the problem by saying "In a few days time we will throw a small feast for family and friends to celebrate your betrothal and make it official. Now I think we should all go to bed as we are all going to be very busy tomorrow."

Cornelia could not sleep. She lay on her bed in the darkness listening to the sounds of the night. A cricket was chirruping loudly in the tree in the garden and was answered by another cricket further away. In the distance an owl hooted. She heard an almost silent footstep in the passage outside and suddenly there was Marcus standing by her bed. He was wearing a simple loincloth, which he dropped, to the floor. He lay down beside her and folded her in his arms.

"I've missed you so much," he said. "I was very relieved to see you come in today and know that you had arrived safely."

He kissed her warmly on the lips and slid his arms around her body. They made love long into the night until eventually Marcus said

"I"d better go back to my own bed," and slipped away as silently as he had come. Cornelia lay in complete happiness and fell asleep with a smile on her lips.

The feast was organised to take place in three days time. Livia and the girls went to the market accompanied by a slave and purchased huge amounts of fruit, vegetables, nuts, fish, meat and baskets of delicious little pastries and sweetmeats. The two days before the feast were spent in frenzied preparations and comings and goings to the bakery to put various meat and fish concoctions in the oven. Marcus was out most of the time during the day visiting friends and summoning them to the feast. He did not repeat his nocturnal visit to Cornelia's bed. He said things would be arranged more satisfactorily after their betrothal had been made official.

On the day of the betrothal after the midday rest Claudia and a slave came into Cornelia's room. Claudia was carrying a saffron coloured robe over her arm and a small tray holding various pots and flasks while the maid was bearing a ewer of warm water. She poured some into the basin on the side table and Claudia added a trickle of perfume from a small flask. The room was filled with the scent of jasmine. They removed Cornelia's everyday robe and the maid, moistening a sponge in the water bathed Cornelia's body from top to toe. She then took a rough linen towel and rubbed her until her skinned took on a rosy glow. Claudia slipped the saffron robe over her head and tied the girdle.

Then as the maid dressed her hair Claudia opened one of the little pots and applied some soft salve to her eyelids and her lips. She looked amongst her collection of pots and opened one containing kohl, but after studying Cornelia's face intently with her head quizzically tilted to the side she said,

"No, I think you look better as you are"

The maid handed Cornelia a silver mirror and as she

surveyed their handiwork she smiled with pleasure.

"Thank you," she said. "I feel marvellous."

"Shall we go down and meet our guests?"

As Claudia and Cornelia entered the atrium Livia and Marcus were standing talking to a dignified lady who though well into middle age was very imposing. Cornelia recognised her as a widow who lived in one of the apartments in their insula. The girls approached the little group and this lady looked at Cornelia and greeted her. Cornelia returned the greeting with a gentle inclination of her head as the lady said to Livia,

"You were right; she is a pretty little thing." Marcus so far had said nothing and when Cornelia looked at him she saw a look of open admiration on his face.

"You look beautiful," he said softly.

Guests arrived and Marcus proudly introduced his betrothed to his friends. A slave handed Cornelia a goblet of sweetened wine and she smiled as she sipped and talked with ease with everyone, basking in the warmth of their admiring looks. A slave approached Livia and spoke softly to her and Livia said, "Dinner is served. Would you all like to come through to the triclinium?"

The meal passed very successfully amidst much stimulating conversation and friendly banter. After the last guest had departed and the family were once more standing in the atrium Marcus said, "Thank you mother, that was a very enjoyable evening."

"I have never enjoyed anything as much," said Cornelia, and she planted a kiss on Livia's cheek and hugged Claudia.

"I'm glad you enjoyed it so much, and now I'm very tired so I shall go to my bed. I'll see you all in the morning," said Livia.

"One moment, before you go mother I have to tell you something. I don't like to cast a cloud on such a perfect evening but I have to leave early tomorrow morning to go to camp to prepare for our departure. I shall be gone before you rise so we should say our "good-byes" now."

Livia and Claudia both hugged Marcus.

"Look after yourself," said his mother.

"I shall miss you," said his sister.

Cornelia said nothing; she just looked at him with sadness. He smiled at her.

"Don't worry," he said, "I'll come and say good bye to you properly before I go, and while I'm away you'll have the wedding to prepare. Before you know it I'll be back."

He was as good as his word. Cornelia had not been in her bed long before he slipped in beside her. They made tender happy love and Cornelia clung to him as if she was to lose him for ever, not just for a few months.

"Don't worry," he said. "I'll come back safely. But I'll tell you one thing."

"What?"

"Before we get married you'll have to arrange for a larger bed."

When Cornelia woke in the morning she was alone and Marcus was gone.

The day to day work of the household continued as normal. The three women went often to the baths together and sometimes strolled through the forum or along the river in the cool of the evening. One evening they took Paulus with them to carry their purchases and as they were crossing the forum a small boy detached himself from grasp of a young man and with a cry of joy flung himself at Paulus. Paulus picked him up and smiling said,

"Hello young man, I thought I told you not to leave go of nurse's hand."

The child laughed and said "I'm not with nurse."

The young man approached and said "I'm sorry for my brother's manners. He seems to have far too much energy for someone so small. Antonius, greet the ladies properly."

"That's all right," said Cornelia."I'm glad to see he has fully recovered from his dip in the Tiber. My slave pulled him out."

"I heard about that." and turning to Paulus he said, "I thank you".

He took control once more of the infant and inclined his head politely at the ladies, then his gaze fixed on Claudia and he stared longer than was necessary.

"Which direction are you going? Perhaps we could walk along with you for a little way?"

"Thank you," said Livia, taking command of the situation. "How do you pass your time here in Rome?" she asked.

"I've only recently returned to Rome. I've been away studying in Athens. But I've finished now and my father is organising a place for me, possibly in the treasury. My mother wanted me to work in the courts and become a lawyer but I much prefer numbers to words."

"I have a son a little older than you who is in the army. He has just left for a tour of duty on the border with Germania. We expect him to be away for some months."

"You must miss him. But his father must be proud of him."

"Yes, he would have been. He, too, was a soldier. But I've been a widow for some years."

The little party strolled along chatting amiably until they arrived at the door of their home.

"Won't you come in and join us for some refreshment before you go home?" said Livia.

"Thank you, we'd love to."

As they entered the house Livia asked a maid to serve some refreshments in the garden. Hector came running up to Cornelia wagging his tail as they stepped into the garden. Little Antonius squealed with delight when he saw the dog and tried to hug him. Hector squirmed in the boy's arms, then turned to lick his face and the boy laughed.

"What's his name?" he asked.

"His name is Hector and he came with me all the way from Britannia," said Cornelia.

Antonius looked wide-eyed.

"Is that far?" he asked.

"Yes, very far. Would you like to play with him?"

"Yes please."

Cornelia picked up a small wooden ball and showed Antonius how to throw it so Hector would bring it back to him.

Paulus had disappeared and Livia was busy offering wine and water to their guest.

"You haven't told us your name." she said, as she handed him a goblet.

"So I haven't," he said. "I'm Quintus, and I'm very pleased to make your acquaintance. But you haven't told me your names either."

"I am Livia and this is my daughter Claudia. That is Cornelia playing with your little brother. She is betrothed to my son."

"And the slave who rescued Antonius?"

"That's Paulus. He came with Cornelia from Britannia."

A maid brought a dish of fruit and Claudia offered this to Quintus who helped himself to an apricot and smiled at her. His teeth bit into the soft flesh but his eyes remained locked on Claudia.

Antonius came running up and threw himself on Quintus.

"I'm thirsty," he said.

Livia poured him a goblet of grape juice and water which he drained in one go.

"My goodness, you were thirsty," she said, and smiling she took a linen napkin and wiped away the purple moustache left by the juice.

"Please may I have a fig?" he asked politely.

"Just one, then we must go home."

As he took his leave they all went to the door and Quintus said to his little brother,

"Come on, up on my back and I'll give you a ride home."

As he hoisted the child onto his back he said

"Thank you for your hospitality, you must let me return it."

"Thank you, that's kind."

The weeks past and no word was heard about Marcus. Cornelia started to feel her days lacked direction and she persuaded Claudia to teach her something of the administration of the insula. She soon grasped the basics of the accounts and one morning, as she was sitting in the atrium adding a column of figures the elderly widow from an apartment on the other side of the block was admitted by Solon.

"Good morning my dear, I was hoping to see Livia, or perhaps Claudia."

"I'm sorry my lady, they are both out. Can I be of any help?"

"Perhaps you can give them a message for me. The hinge of one of my shutters has broken and I am unable to open it for fear of it falling in the street."

"Oh dear, what a nuisance. I will send someone round right away. Can I offer you some refreshment while we wait?"

"A cool drink would be very welcome, it is very hot today."

Cornelia clapped her hands and Solon appeared as if by magic.

"Solon, can you arrange a cool drink for our visitor and would you please find Paulus and tell him to bring his tools and accompany her back to her apartment to fix her shutter?"

Solon went out and a maid soon arrived bearing a goblet of cool cordial brewed from hibiscus flowers. A few moments later Paulus appeared bearing a bag of tools.

"Thank you my dear," said the matron. "I'm glad to see you are settling in so well," and she departed with Paulus following.

Cornelia felt she could probably manage the work of running the building quite well and looked forward to showing Marcus how useful she would be as his wife. There was also the question of Claudia. She and Quintus had met on more than one occasion and it was plain to see that the feelings they had for each other were more than friendship. Quintus had now started work in the Treasury and Cornelia felt sure it would not be long before he would be approaching Livia formally to request the hand of her daughter in marriage.

This would mean that Livia would need Cornelia to take over the work done by Claudia. Cornelia idly wondered who would be married first, she or Claudia.

In her reverie she suddenly started to think of her own mother. Although she had thought of her often since leaving home as the months went by she thought of Britannia less often. She wondered if it would be possible to send a letter to her family and how long it would take to get there. Perhaps she would write to them after she was married.

Chapter Seven

One morning a few days later Cornelia awoke and as she opened her eyes an urgent feeling of nausea overwhelmed her. She lay thinking about it for no more than a few seconds then leaped from her bed and vomited into the chamber pot. She did not feel ill, on the contrary, she felt as fit as she usually did. She then had to admit to herself that what she had suspected for the past three or four weeks must if fact be true; she was with child. She did not see how she could keep this from Livia but she was glad that she was officially betrothed to Marcus and that he would probably be home before her condition became evident to the world at large.

She rinsed out her mouth and washed her face and slipping into her robe and sandals she made her way to the atrium. The hallway was empty, as was the triclinium and she heard voices coming from the garden. She stepped out into the sunshine and found Livia and Claudia partaking of breakfast under the pergola. She joined them and greeting them with a smile she helped herself to a plate of fruit as the maid poured her a tumbler of pomegranate juice.

"Did you sleep well my dear?" asked Livia. "You look a trifle pale."

"Yes, very well, thank you. I have something to tell you."

"And we have something to tell you," said Claudia.

"Have you news of Marcus?" she said excitedly.

"Alas, no," said Livia.

"What mother wants to tell you is that Quintus has asked to be betrothed to me," said Claudia smiling broadly.

"I can tell from your face that the idea is not entirely repulsive to you," said Cornelia.

Everyone laughed and Cornelia asked

"When do you plan to marry?"

"Well, I would like Marcus to be present, as the one male in the family, so we are going to wait two or three months and see if there is any possibility of his coming home, even just for a short while. Who knows? He could be home even sooner. These frontier skirmishes usually don't last too long."

"I must say I am very happy that you are here to help me with the management," said Livia, smiling fondly at Cornelia.

Claudia remembered Cornelia's opening remark.

"What was it you wanted to tell us?" she asked.

"It's just that I am with child."

"Oh, that's wonderful," said Claudia.

"I thought you were," said Livia.

"How did you guess? I've only been sure myself for about two weeks."

"Let's put it down to an older woman"s experience, and the fact that for the past few weeks you have had a certain look about you, a certain radiance."

"Well I have to say I didn't feel particularly radiant when I awoke this morning. I was horribly sick."

"Don't worry, that will pass," said Livia.

A few days later Livia asked Cornelia to go to the market for a supply of paper. She was accompanied by Paulus. It was a sunny morning as they strolled down the hill to the Forum. The brilliant sky was high and cloudless, presaging a hot day. Cornelia looked around at the city, admiring the buildings and watching the busy toings and froings of the early morning crowds. She and Paulus turned into a side alley in which a flight of steps led down to the square. Cornelia was feeling elated by her surroundings and the general atmosphere of bustle around her. She took the last few steps in a series of skips and jumps.

"You shouldn't do that in your condition," said Paulus.

Cornelia turned and looked at him, surprised.

"What do you know about my condition?" she said.

"I heard the slave who empties your chamber pot talking to the kitchen slave. As you seem undoubtedly very well it wasn't difficult to deduce why you are sick almost every morning."

"Oh."

They walked on in silence until Paulus asked

"Are you pleased?"

"Of course I am," Cornelia answered.

"Will you send a letter to your parents and tell them they are to have a grandchild?"

Cornelia thought about it for a while then said,

"Yes, I will. But I think I shall wait until after the wedding so that they can see that I am living as a respectable married woman, then they won't feel so bad about the fact that I ran away."

It would not be fair to say that she was entirely self-centred, in fact she often thought of her family in Britain, usually with a sense of guilt, but her life was driven by the desires of youth and the excitement that every day brought and she always told herself she would write home later.

The necessary purchase was accomplished and Paulus took the parcel and they made their way back up the hill. They entered the house and went into the study where Paulus placed the packet of paper on the writing table and left the room. Livia was seated behind the table adding a row of figures.

"How are you dear?" she asked Cornelia. "How were things in the Forum?"

"Hot and getting hotter," she replied as she slumped down in a basket chair.

At that moment a slave entered the room and said,

"My lady, a soldier is here to speak to you."

"Maybe he has news from Marcus," said Livia as she rose and made her way to the atrium.

The soldier was older than Marcus and did not look like a fighting man.

"My lady, I come from the secretary of the cavalry unit's office." The man was clearly ill at ease about something. "I have a message for you from the unit's commander. Alas it is my sad duty to inform you that your son was killed in battle two weeks ago."

Cornelia heard the words and suddenly a loud buzzing filled her ears and she fell to the floor in a dead faint.

Paulus was summoned and he carried her to her chamber and laid her gently on the bed. She lay for a night and a day while Claudia and Livia tended to her needs. From time to time she seemed to wake but she did not seem to recognise her surroundings and the words she mumbled made no coherent sense. On the evening of the second day she opened her eyes and though the expression in them was dull she was once more aware of her surroundings and those around her. Then the memory of the soldier and his news flooded back into her mind. Desolation and emptiness filled her soul. She turned nervously to Livia.

"It's true, isn't it?" she said.

"Yes dear it's true," said Livia and though her eyes were dry her voice was flat expressionless.

Claudia came in. Her eyes were red from weeping.

"Here," said Livia, "drink this," and she held a beaker to her lips. It contained wine and water sweetened with honey.

"I'll get cook to make you some soup," said Claudia, and went out of the room.

"I'm not hungry, I couldn't eat a thing."

"Never mind, just try. You have to try and regain your strength."

"For the baby?"

Livia seemed to pause, and glanced at Claudia, before turning back to Cornelia. "I'm sorry dear, you have lost the baby."

Cornelia looked at her as if struggling to understand what she had said then suddenly she started to weep. The tears ran down her face and she was wracked by sobs that seemed to come from the depth of her being.

Livia put an arm around her shoulders and comforted her as only a mother could. Cornelia did not want to know. She just stared at the wall. Marcus gone. The baby gone. Her life was pointless, empty and pitiful. She thought of her mother and how much she would have enjoyed being a grandmother, and uncontrollable sobs wracked her body. Eventually the sobs diminished and by the time Claudia returned bearing a bowl of soup Cornelia was able to swallow some of it and even eat some small sippets of bread soaked in it. Then she turned to stare at the wall again and the pain came flooding back as tears rolled unheeded down her cheeks. Livia sat with her for while, then quietly slipped out of the room.

Unnoticed by Cordelia the sun crept across the sky, then sank to disappear behind the rooftops of Rome. Cordelia's room darkened to match her bleak mood. Eventually she slipped into a fitful sleep. She awoke in the dark once, then she slept soundly and next morning, looking rather pale, she appeared for breakfast. As she walked onto the loggia Livia looked up and said,

"Good morning dear. How are you feeling?"

"Much better, thank you," said Cordelia, though it was not true. She felt terrible, but she forced a thin smile. "I think I should eat something now."

Livia offered her some apricot puree preserved in honey and some soft bread made with milk. When Cornelia had eaten enough she said to Livia,

"I want to apologise."

"For what?"

"Since the messenger came from the army with the news about Marcus I have thought of nothing but what his death means to me. You have lost a son yet you did not breakdown. I have also lost what might have been a son . You, Claudia, have lost a brother. I have a brother and I know what I would feel if I lost him. I am sorry."

The other two women looked at her for a few moments as if they did not know how to respond, Livia said "You do not need to feel like that. It was not your fault Marcus was killed. His father also died in battle and even though my heart sank when Marcus said he wanted to become a soldier I knew I would never try and stop him and I also knew that soldiering being the dangerous occupation it is there was a strong possibility that I would lose him as I lost his father. In fact I am grateful to you that you gave him the happiness you did. It's a pity he did not know about the baby, he would have been very proud, but please don't feel in any way responsible. That's the Fates at work. I want you to know that you can stay here for as long as you wish and I will always look upon you as another daughter."

"And I as your sister," said Claudia.

"Thank you," said Cornelia blinking away her tears.

"Now, let's see if we can't bring some roses back to your cheeks, you look like a marble statue."

As the weeks went by Cornelia's health improved but her old cheerful spirit did not return. She spent time each morning with Claudia over the administration of the apartment block. She went with her to make any purchases necessary and she accompanied both Livia and Claudia to the baths two or three times a week. One day as they were lounging in the pool Cornelia said to Claudia

"Have you fixed a day for your wedding yet?"

"No, we felt we wanted to wait a while out of respect for Marcus."

"I think we should start to plan it. It will be something to look forward to."

The next half hour was spent in discussions about dresses and hairstyles and went on to food and table arrangements and guest lists. The next day, when Quintus called Claudia told him she was ready to fix their wedding day. He was overjoyed and they sat down and wrote out a list of guests which he would be inviting. When Claudia saw some of the names on the list she trembled inwardly at the level of importance of many of them.

"Don't worry," said Quintus when he noticed her apprehension, "most of them are very ordinary when you get to know them. Everything will be fine."

On the day of the wedding the main doorway of the house was decorated with branches of greenery and flowers intertwined with coloured ribbons and carpets were laid on the doorstep and into the hallway. Claudia appeared dressed in her white marriage tunic with the traditional flame-coloured veil held in place on her head with a garland of flowers. Quintus gazed at his bride in admiration and they talked softly together while the marriage contract was signed and witnessed. When this was done an aunt of Quintus's took both Claudia and Quintus by the hand and joined their hands together while the bride and groom looked into each other's eyes and silently made their vows before the assembly. Once these formalities were over all the guests wished the couple good luck and the wedding feast began. There were so many people that they could not possibly fit in to the triclinium so tables and couches had be set up all around the atrium. During the course of the meal some of Quintus's friends exchanged ribald jokes and songs were sung.

Eventually there was a banging on the street door and it was opened to reveal a band of flute players and a group of boys bearing torches. They had come to accompany the bride to her new home. Claudia went towards her mother and hugged her warmly. Although tradition decreed she show a maidenly reluctance to leave her childhood home the warmth she gave the hug was genuine.

"Thank you, mother, for everything," she said and Quintus pulled her from her mother's arms. Before she left her mother handed her the traditional spindle and three small coins, one for Quintus, one for the gods at the crossroads and one for the household gods in her new home. One of the torch bearers lit a branch from the kitchen hearth and led the procession that took Claudia to her new life. When they arrived at the big house that was to be her home She smeared the doorpost with lard and decked it with wool, then her friends picked her up and carried her across the threshold. Quintus then firmly shut the door behind him.

At this point the unmarried men among the guests repaired to a tavern to carry on drinking the health of the happy couple. Livia accepted the thanks of the other guests, who climbed into their chairs that had followed the procession and were carried home. Livia and Cornelia walked home lit by Solon carrying a torch and followed by Paulus. When they arrived home most of the remains of the feast had already been cleared away by the slaves. Livia and Cornelia went into the study. Cornelia suddenly felt as if life had gone flat but Livia suddenly put her head down on her writing table and wept. Cornelia, amazed at this display of grief rushed around to the other side of the table and put her hand on Livia's back and gently stroked it.

"What's the matter?" she asked. "Why are you sad?"

"I'm not really sad," she answered, drying her eyes on a linen square. "It's just that all my children are gone now."

"Claudia hasn't really gone. You will see her again."

"That's true. Forgive me, I'm just a silly old woman. I think we should go to bed now. It's been a very full day."

As the weeks went by Cornelia was able to do more and more of the administration on the insula. It was not work she approached with happy anticipation but as the weeks went by she found it easier and she felt it was her duty to help Livia all she could. Claudia called frequently and both Livia and Cornelia were invited to the big house on the hill. Claudia had taken to being the mistress of the house without too much difficulty. The senator, Quintus's father, had lost his wife with the birth of Antonius and although the household was run efficiently by the major domo and his band of slaves Quintus was very glad to have a wife who could act as hostess for the parties and receptions that were a necessary part of political life. Claudia had been married about ten weeks when a slave from her household arrived at the insula with a note for Livia and Cornelia. It was from Claudia asking them if they would like to meet her that afternoon at the baths.

The weather had become insufferably hot and the thought

of immersing themselves in the cool water was very enticing. When they arrived at the changing room with their slave they found Claudia already there. Her slave was folding her clothes and placing them in the cubicle. When all three were undressed they went through to the room where masseurs were waiting with scented oils and strigils. After the grime of the day had been removed and they were sitting in the tepid bath Claudia said "I have a proposition. Well actually I have some news and a proposition."

The other two looked at expectantly.

"I expect you can guess my news, I am almost certainly pregnant."

"That's wonderful," said Livia.

"I hope everything goes well," said Cornelia.

"Thank you, that's very kind of you considering your own misfortune. I was a bit worried about telling you. I didn't want to upset you."

"That's all right, I'm not upset," and she realised that she actually wasn't upset.

"Now for my proposition. Mother, now that you are virtually alone there seems little point in hanging on to the insula. Quintus and I would like you to come and live with us. The house is very large and you will have your own apartment and when the baby comes you will be a great help. Of course we will have a nursemaid so you wouldn't have to do any work but a Grandmother is far superior to a nursemaid for teaching manners and playing games and telling stories. Of course Cornelia can come as your companion. Don't make a decision now, but I would like you to think about it."

A week later Livia was still thinking about it. Claudia's proposition made sense. Her husband was dead, her son was dead, so there was no one to inherit. Claudia had married well and had no need of any financial help, and the idea of having a little one to spoil was a very tempting thought. She decided to make some enquiries and see how much she could get for the insula. It was very well built and well maintained, it had no major flaws and was not likely to collapse as some tall blocks did.

Cornelia also gave the proposition some thought. To live in such a luxurious house was tempting. To be in a position to socialise with an elevated section of society was also tempting. She also felt that her decision might somehow affect Livia's decision. She turned the pros and cons over in her mind for some days and her decision, when it came, surprised even herself.

The relentless summer heat showed no sign of abating when one afternoon, after the midday meal when the house was quietly somnolent she climbed to the top of the building in search of Paulus. She had never been up to this floor. It was as clean as the rest of the house but the rooms were much smaller. She knocked on a door at the end of the passage and it was opened by Paulus. He looked at her with surprise.

"Is something wrong?"

"No, I just want to talk to you."

"Come in," and he stood back to allow her to enter.

The room was small and sparsely but adequately furnished.

"By Jupiter, it's hot in here. How on earth do you sleep?,

"I don't. When it's as hot as this I take a blanket and go down and sleep in the garden, usually with Hector."

"I didn't know," said Cornelia. She realised that since coming to Rome there were a lot of things she didn't know about Paulus.

"You said you wanted to talk to me. Was it about something special?"

"Yes," she said, "it is. Paulus, I want to go home."

Paulus looked at her in amazement then gradually a look of deep happiness came into his eyes and gradually extended to his open mouth which spread into a smile.

"I was beginning to think I would never hear those words."

"Won't you mind leaving Rome? It's such a beautiful city with so much going on and so much to do."

"Both of those things are true, but when you've seen the games half a dozen times they"re not interesting any more. The countryside is beautiful but not in the same way as the countryside in Britain. Britain is home. It's where my father is, and where your family is. Apart from which it's as hot as Hades in this roof."

"It certainly is. Shall we go down to the garden?"

"Let's go down to the river, it might be cooler down there."

The perspiration was running down Cornelia's thighs and her tunic was sticking to her back. As they approached the Tiber a very slight breeze was blowing up the river coming in with the rising tide.

"When do you want to go? Paulus asked.

"Soon. This evening I shall talk to Livia about it, then tomorrow we'll probably go up and see Claudia. After that there really isn't any reason to delay.

"Would you like to see Phoebe in Ostia before we leave We can probably get a ship from there."

"That's a wonderful suggestion," said Cornelia, and suddenly she started to feel excited about going home. Her old thirst for life seemed to be returning.

Telling Livia of her decision proved to be much easier that she anticipated.

"I can quite understand your decision. You must miss your parents and your home and while you remain in Rome you will constantly be reminded of the unhappy things that have happened to you here. When will you leave?"

"As soon as possible. Paulus says we should get well on our way before the winter comes. We will go to Ostia and visit Phoebe before we depart."

Livia crossed to a cupboard in the corner of the office and took out a wooden box. Taking a key that was fastened to her girdle she unlocked it and gave Cornelia a handful of coins of various worth.

"This is for your journey," she said.

Cornelia took the money and said

"Thank you, and thank you for all you have done for me. I am glad you have decided to go and live with Claudia. When you no longer have the insula you will not need help, and I'm sure Claudia will be glad of your help with her baby."

"I wish you a safe journey. I'm sure you will be well protected by Paulus. I ask you only one thing."

"What's that?"

"When you arrive safely home send me a letter telling me how you are."

"Of course I will," and the two women embraced each other fondly.

That evening Paulus accompanied them to see Claudia and say their "Good-byes" Antonius came running to Paulus who picked him up and said

"Now be a good boy, and no more jumping into rivers, at least not until you can swim."

His father took Paulus by the hand and said

"Thank you for saving my son. Good luck on your journey."

"Thank you, sir".

Cornelia embraced Claudia and wished her good luck with the baby.

As the trio departed the family waved from the doorway.

Early next morning, as soon as they had broken their fast Cornelia and Paulus set off down the hill to the river. Hector walked closely to Cornelia's heels, trotting along with great purpose with his tongue lolling from his mouth. Cornelia looked at him and laughed.

"He seems to know we're going somewhere special. He almost looks as if he's grinning.," she said.

Arriving at the quayside it was very easy to find a barge that was going down to Ostia. Once on board they stood on the deck and watched the city slipping by.

"Any regrets?" asked Paulus.

"No, I don't think so. I wonder how things are at home."

"If all goes well we should be home in time for the harvest," said Paulus.

They stood silently, each preoccupied with his own thoughts. Cornelia thought about her family with fondness and a longing to be re-united, but with a little nagging doubt that her father might be less than pleased at her departure from home.

When they arrived in Ostia they made their way to the house of Hermione. As they stepped into the courtyard they saw Phoebe cleaning the top of a dining table. She had her back to them and as she turned Cornelia noticed that she was pregnant once more. She exclaimed with delight when her gaze fell upon the visitors and rushed over to embrace them. Alerted by the joyous greetings a little boy came running out from the house and gazed up at Paulus and Cornelia from the safety of his mother's skirts.

Phoebe picked him up and said to him,

"Say hello to our visitors. This is Paulus who is very special to you, and this is my good friend Cornelia."

The child smiled and raised a chubby little hand. At that moment Philip appeared in the doorway. He looked well and happy but Cornelia and Paulus noticed that his right arm was missing from just above the elbow. They all greeted one another warmly.

"I'm sorry about your arm," said Cornelia.

"I'm not," said Philip with a smile. "You can't be a one-armed soldier so I've been discharged. I have a small pension from the army and with what we make here we live very comfortably."

Turning to Cornelia he said,

"I was luckier that Marcus. Please accept my sympathies. He died very bravely and very quickly. I was there, and can tell you about it if you like. "

"Thank you," said Cornelia. The two sat down to talk.

"You must be parched," said Phoebe and she disappeared

towards the kitchen. She returned accompanied by Hermione and Philip's sisters who were bearing goblets and a pitcher of wine. They sat under the canopy of vines until late in the day exchanging news as they ate and drank. Then Philip went with Paulus down to the harbour to search for a ship that was sailing the next day towards Gaul.

They finally lighted upon a large cargo ship that sat low in the water and was obviously loaded ready to sail.

The captain was standing on the quayside directing final operations. He was a short, stocky man with a swarthy complexion that suited his occupation. He had light creases at the sides of his eyes from screwing them up against the glare as he looked into the distance at sea. He stood with his feet slightly apart and firmly planted on the dock The muscles on his arms were big and strong and he exuded a comfortable air of self worth They approached him to see if he would take two passengers and a dog. Paulus explained that though he was not an experienced sailor he was willing to work for his passage in any capacity that the captain could use him.

"You look fit enough and we can always do with an extra pair of hands, especially in the case of a strong blow." A deal was struck and coins changed hands.

"We sail at first light so be here early."

"Perhaps it would be better if we came aboard tonight?" said Paulus.

The captain agreed to this proposal.

"I will fetch the others and our baggage and return before nightfall," and with a clasp of hands to seal the deal Paulus and Philip returned to the eating house.

The sun was just making itself seen above the horizon when the ship slipped its moorings and slid out of the harbour. Cornelia was standing on the deck with Hector seated at her feet. Paulus was heaving on ropes to hoist the sail along with other deckhands when Cornelia heard their names called from the shore. There on the quayside stood Philip with Paulinus on his shoulders and his good arm around Phoebe's waist. Paulinus and Phoebe were waving and shouting their farewells. Paulus paused in his work to wave a hand and Cornelia responded to the goodbyes with moist eyes. Hector barked and wagged his tail. She stood at the rail until the little party on the shore were nothing more than dots.

"Well Hector," she said, "let's look to the future."

Cornelia had been allocated a sleeping space which doubled as a rope and sail store. She had a straw mattress on top of coils of rope which actually proved to be fairly comfortable and it was situated next to the area where the ship's cook had his fire. This made it a bit hot and stuffy during the day but at night, although the stove was allowed to die down, the accumulated warmth of the day made her little cubby hole quite warm. Paulus slept with the crew, either below decks in amongst the cargo or out on deck if the night was hot. After three days they could see a sizeable port but the captain showed no sign of approaching the shore.

"Where's that?" Cornelia asked a sailor.

"That's Massilia," he said. "We're not going there this time, we'll call there on the way back."

"Then where are we going?" she asked.

"Further along the coast, to Narbo."

That evening as she and Paulus were sitting on deck eating a bowl of stew each she said.

"Apparently we are going to somewhere called Narbo."

"Yes," said Paulus. "Colonia Narbo Martius, to give it its proper name. It is a few miles further west along the coast."

"How do we get home from there"

"It depends."

"On what?"

"On what we find when we get there."

The winds were favourable and two days later they approached the land where the buildings of a town could be seen. As they neared the harbour the sail was dropped and

Paulus helped the crew to man the oars as they glided gently up to the dockside. When the ship was safely tied up the captain approached Paulus.

"What do you plan to do now?" he asked.

"I'm not sure. It would be best if we could find some soldiers going north but there might not be any. We might find some other travellers. I think we'll go to an inn and see if anyone is travelling in our direction. Where are you going now?"

"We've got cargo to unload here and then we sail on into the ocean to Gades. We unload the rest there and take on another load before going back to Rome."

"Would you advise us to go with you to Gades?"

"No, not that I haven't valued your help, but it's nearer to the northern shores from here. If I were you, I would head northwest to the western coast at Burdigala. If you get there you'll find a ship going to Britannia. They ship a lot of wine from there."

They bade the captain goodbye and the little trio made their way into the town. As they passed through the market square they came across a cart laden with amphorae of wine which pulled up outside an inn. They entered the inn to seek food and possibly beds for the night. A little slave was helping the wine merchant to unload the amphorae and carry them into the inn. As he staggered under the weight of the heavy jars Paulus went up to him and lifted a jar effortlessly.

"Where do you want this?" he said to the innkeeper.

The innkeeper indicated the storage room and the load safely stowed he thanked Paulus.

"That deserves a drink young man, sit down with your good lady," and he instructed the slave to serve them. The wine merchant joined them and thanking Paulus for his helped he asked him what he was doing in Narbo.

"Because," he said,"you don't sound as if you come from these parts."

"Indeed we do not. We have just arrived from Rome and

are travelling north. We are hoping we might find a troop of soldiers or a large party going in that direction."

"I don't think there are any soldiers on the move at the moment. I usually get to hear if there are. Some of the local troops come in here from time to time," said the inn-keeper.

"I'm setting off north early tomorrow morning," said the wine merchant "I"d be glad of your company. You can stay the night at the vineyard and maybe you'll find a party of travellers after that."

"Thank you sir," said Paulus. During this conversation Cornelia had sat silent. For once she was content to let Paulus organise their affairs and did not feel the need to make it plain to everyone that he was her slave. The inn keeper showed them a small room under the eves and it was at this point that Paulus himself explained the situation.

"I shall be happy to sleep in the loft above the storeroom," he said.

Next morning saw them aboard the wine merchant's cart. Cornelia was in a corner of the cart safely wedged in with their bundles with Hector at her side. Paulus sat next to the driver and the two men talked about horses and oxen and compared notes on the different lives they led, one growing crops and tending animals and the other growing vines and making wine.

When the sun was at its height they stopped at the roadside for a simple meal while Cornelia stretched her legs. Then they were off again. Evening saw them arriving at a long, low building amongst fields of vines.

The men unhitched the two oxen from the cart and led them into an enclosure then they all went into the house. Over dinner they discussed their forthcoming journey.

"The next big town is Tolosa. You should get there in about three days. They bring wine down to Narbonnensis and often go back with salt. Once you arrive in Burdigala you should have no difficulty finding a boat to Britannia. Most of the way there passes through wine growing country and a lot of wine is shipped out of Burdigala. I thought of selling wine there as the price is higher but I decided it's too far. I'm not getting any younger.,

"What are the roads like?" asked Paulus.

"Not bad and usually quite safe, and we should have good travelling weather over the next week."

In spite of the fact that Cornelia had spent most of the day riding in the back of the cart the good meal and even better wine she had consumed coupled with the comforting drone of the men"s voices lulled her into a soporific state and she felt her eyelids drooping.

"Someone's tired," said their host, smiling. Cornelia was shown to a room where she fell asleep even before her head had touched the pillow.

Chapter Eight

They journeyed happily for the next two days. The weather was kind and even the nights were warm enough not to need to seek shelter. After two days the provisions they had brought with them were exhausted but they came upon a wayside inn. They still had money left from the coins that Livia had given to them and entered the inn like the confident seasoned travellers that they had become. The room had a number of travellers in it. A family were seated around a table eating and in a corner were a group of three men drinking wine. The men looked up when Cornelia and Paulus came in. Cornelia did not like the way one of the men stared at her. Paulus approached the inn-keeper and asked if they could have a meal and a bed for the night. When the meal was served the inn-keeper lingered at their table.

"Have you come far?"

"Yes, from Rome," said Cornelia.

"I thought you weren't from here. Have you got far to go?"

Before Cornelia could volunteer any further information Paulus quickly said

"Tomorrow we're going to Tolosa, we have relatives there," and he looked to Cornelia as if to say "Don't say anything".

Later, when they were shown to a room Paulus said "I think I will sleep in here tonight. I didn't like the look of those men downstairs. If I sleep on the floor against the door we can't be taken by surprise."

They both fell asleep almost immediately but after about an hour Paulus was awaked by a very low soft growl from Hector. He put his hand on the dog's head to calm him and noticed the latch of the door slowly and silently returning to its closed position. Someone had tried to enter the room but had also probably heard Hector's warning and thought better of it.

Next morning they were up early but found that the group of men of the evening before had already gone. Paulus purchased provisions from the inn-keeper and they set off as soon as possible. The inn-keeper said they would certainly reach Tolosa before nightfall. As the day progressed Cornelia chatted in her normal, talkative way but by late afternoon she gradually became aware that Paulus was not contributing to the conversation and indeed he looked a trifle uneasy. After he had looked over his shoulder for the third time in ten minutes she asked him what was bothering him.

"I think we're being followed."

"Really, by whom?"

"I'm not sure but I didn't like the look of those men in the inn last night".

Suddenly, as if on cue, a man leapt out of the bushes at the side of the road and stood in front of them holding a knife.

"Hand over your money and you won't get hurt," he said with a sardonic smile on his face.

Cornelia recognised one of the men from the previous night. Paulus pulled his own knife from his belt and dropping his bundle where he stood he stepped forward.

"Oh, so you want to fight," said the robber.

Paulus and the man eyed each other and circled warily. As the couple turned and the man had his back to Cornelia she suddenly sprang forward and kicked him as hard as she could in the crutch. The man gave a bellow and dropping his knife he fell to the ground clutching his groin. Cornelia grabbed his knife just as Paulus shouted "Look out!"

Suddenly she found herself grabbed around the neck from behind by a strong arm. Hector, seeing his beloved mistress being attacked leapt for the man"s throat and dug his teeth in. The attacker staggered back with blood spurting from his neck. Cornelia called Hector who came to her side and stood looking at the man with the fur on his back standing up and a deep growl in his throat. Suddenly the third man appeared and aimed a kick at Hector who yelped in pain. At this

Cornelia forgot her fear and felt only rage. She went for the attacker with the knife she was still holding and managed to cut him badly in the wrist before he was able to disarm her. Meanwhile the man she had kicked had recovered sufficiently to rise and gave Paulus a hefty blow in the ribs. Paulus turned pale but looking the man in the eye he said "Unless you all give up I shall have no hesitation in sticking this knife in your guts."

At this point the men decided the fight was proving more difficult than they had anticipated and decided to abandon it. They gathered themselves together and helping their companion with the neck wound they slunk off in to the undergrowth. Paulus still looked very white and was shaking.

"Are you all right?" asked Cornelia.

"I think so. Let's get away from here as quickly as possible."

Paulus picked up his bundle but when he tried to swing it onto his shoulder he winced. Instead he carried it under his arm and in his other hand he carried his knife at the ready. They walked on slowly like this for the next hour until the buildings of a town came into view. They stopped at the first inn they came to and as they entered Paulus fell into a dead faint on the floor.

The inn keeper came forward at Cornelia's cry and seeing the white-faced Paulus on the floor tried to raise him into a sitting position. At the movement Paulus groaned. The inn-keeper's wife came forward and put a goblet of neat wine to his lips. His eyelids flickered open and he sipped the wine. The colour slowly returned to his face and he staggered to his feet and sank onto a chair that was offered to him.

"What happened?" asked the inn-keepers wife.

"Some men attacked us on the road," said Cornelia. "They wanted to rob us but we fought."

"Where are you going?"

"We're on our way home."

"Where's home?"

"Britannia."

"Britannia! Well you won't be going to Britannia for a day or two, at least not until our friend here is better. You can stay here. Have you got money?"

"Yes, we have enough to pay for lodging for a while."

That night Paulus slept in the bed on Cornelia's instructions and she made herself as comfortable as she could on the floor. Hector slept at the door. After Cornelia had been asleep for a while she was awaked by Paulus who was talking in his sleep. His words were garbled and completely unintelligible. It was still dark so she decided she had not been asleep for long. She rose and went to the side of the bed but it was too dark to see anything so she went over to the window and opened the shutters. By the feeble light that entered she could see that Paulus was still asleep but his head was tossing from side to side. She reached out and touched his head to find it was bathed in perspiration and felt abnormally hot. She took a cloth from her bundle and wetting it at the pitcher of water she wiped his face and smoothed back his hair. She knelt beside the bed and looking at his tormented face she suddenly felt a fear she had never experienced before. Paulus had always been there, strong and reliable and ready to do her bidding. Suddenly it occurred to her that she might have to take charge and that Paulus would not be able to help. She watched over him through the night and eventually fell asleep sitting on the floor resting her head on her arm on the edge of the bed. As dawn crept through the open shutters she awoke feeling cramped to see that Paulus was lying still. In a moment of horror she thought he was dead but placing her hand on his forehead found he was warm and in fact was sleeping peacefully. She decided to take Hector outside so she could stretch her legs and they could both answer the call of nature. When they returned she found Paulus awake.

"Hello," she said. "How are you feeling?"

"Much better but I ache abominably. I think that thug broke a rib when he hit me. I'll recover."

"I think we"d better rest her for a day or two until you feel fit enough to travel. I'll go and see the inn-keeper and see what I can arrange."

Suddenly Cornelia felt capable once more now that she knew that Paulus was recovering.

She went to speak to the inn-keeper and explained the situation. She knew that their enforced stay would make serious inroads into their finances but decided that if the worse came to the worse she could probably sell one of her brooches. A slave was sent to attend to Paulus's personal needs and the inn-keeper's wife brewed a handful of herbs in water, added a spoon of honey and told Cornelia to give him the resultant concoction from time to time through the day to dull the pain. By the evening Paulus felt well enough to rise from his bed and join everyone in the main room for dinner. Cornelia made no remarks about his being her slave and was happy for him to eat with everyone else. After dinner Paulus said he would be happy to sleep in the hayloft and Cornelia slept comfortably in the bedroom. As she fell asleep she wondered at her emotions when Paulus was ill, after all he was only a slave, but then she realised he was more that just a slave, he was part of her life, her childhood, her home. Suddenly she realised how much she was longing to see her home again, to embrace her parents and hug her big brother. She fell asleep wondering how the colt was doing that had been born just before she had left and whether this year's harvest would be a good one.

Next morning, after that had broken their fast on fresh bread and sweet milk the inn-keeper's wife gave Paulus a small jar of the brew for his pain and suggested he might feel more comfortable if she bound his ribs firmly with a length of linen. When he lifted his tunic he displayed a large bruise where he had been punched. Everyone was horrified.

"He certainly gave you a hard thump", said their host.

"He certainly did", said Paulus. "But you should have seen the damage we did to them".

They said their farewells and set off towards the town centre.

"I think," said Paulus, "that we should go by cart from now on. Unless we could find a large group travelling we would probably be safer on a cart. We will have to look for a merchant."

Cornelia agreed and they made for the centre of the small town. The market was easy to find and there was a surprisingly large number of carts getting ready to leave in both directions. They found one going north and hailed the driver.

"How far are you going?" asked Paulus.

"Burdigala," replied the man.

"Will you take two passenger?"

"And a dog," added Cornelia.

"Will you pay or do you want to work?"

"We would rather pay. How much?"

The sum quoted by the carter seemed a little high but when they demurred he pointed out that the fare included one hot meal every evening the deal was struck.

Cornelia clambered up first swiftly followed by Hector. Paulus tossed their bundles up and then jumped on. As he landed he winced slightly.

"I think this is the best way to travel at present, at least until my ribs heal and I can look after your safety."

"Thank you Paulus," said Cornelia, and she realised that she was genuinely grateful for his consideration for their safety. Paulus was somewhat surprised. She had never thanked him before, not for anything he might have done for her. She had always taken everything for granted.

Their journey to Burdigala was long but uneventful. Sometimes they rode on the cart and sometimes they walked alongside to stretch their legs. Paulus's ribs gradually gave him less pain and the bruising disappeared. By the time they arrived at the port he was fit enough to help in unloading the cargo of salt. They stood in the market bidding farewell to their travelling companions.

"Thank you for your help," said the carter, patting Paulus on the shoulder.

"You've got a grand man here lady," he said and smiled at Cornelia.

She opened her mouth to point out that Paulus was her slave and not her man but then thought better of it and just smiled.

They shouldered their bundles and closely followed by Hector they made their way towards the port where they could see the masts of large ships bobbing gently by the wharves. Most of the ships were either loading or unloading but Paulus stopped near one with the minimum activity on board. The ship sat low in the water and he deduced that it was probably ready to sail.

"Hallo aboard!" he called from the quayside.

A boy of no more that twelve who was sitting on the deck scraping carrots looked up.

"When do you sail?" asked Paulus.

"With tonight's tide," said the boy.

"Where do you go?" asked Paulus.

"Portus Ardaoni in Britannia."

Cornelia's heart gave a little jump at the sound of her home country. Soon they would be home and she would see her family again.

"Can we see the Master?"

"Just a minute," replied the boy and sticking his head down a hatch in the deck he called, "Father, some people to see you."

A face that was an older version of the child's appeared in the hatchway.

"I'm the Master, what's your business?" the face said.

"We seek passage to Britannia."

"We sail tonight, we cannot wait."

"We're ready, we can board now."

"You look like a strong sort of chap. Ever worked on a ship?"

"Yes sir."

The master looked at him for a few seconds then briefly glanced at Cornelia and Hector and made a decision.

"O.K. Come aboard."

Cornelia was shown a space in a locker full of spare ropes where she could place her bedroll while Paulus went below to the area where the crew slept. The ship had a sturdy mast and rolled along a boom was a quantity of thick brown canvas that comprised the sail. There was a bank of oars on each side with two men to an oar. The young lad was showing them around.

"They're just for getting into and out of harbour. Once we're at sea we raise the sail. On this trip there will be plenty of wind, it's always a quick trip at this season."

He was not exaggerating! The crew manned the oars and as the ship nosed its way towards the mouth of the harbour the cook prepared the dinner. As soon as they were away from the shelter of the estuary the oars were shipped and the crew busied themselves unfurling and hoisting the sail. As the sail filled the ship tilted to one side and, settling itself at what Cornelia thought was a precarious angle it seemed to leap forward like a horse that had been spurred. The Master was at the steering oar while a few sailors who obviously knew what they were about tended and trimmed the sails. The rest of the crew took their places on deck with their backs lodged against the side-rails or various hatch covers or the mast itself. When all were safely seated the cook came round with a pot from which he ladled a portion of stew into each man"s bowl while the boy followed with a basket of bread. Paulus, who had already been pressed into service went round with a jar of wine and water. When everyone was served Paulus and the boy took their places.

Before eating Paulus came to Cornelia and handed her his bowl and chunk of bread then went to get another for himself.

"I'm not sure whether I'm really hungry," she said as the ship creamed along and jumped over the wave tops with little bumps.

"Try and eat it and then go straight to sleep. You'll feel better in the morning." So saying he returned to his space on deck.

In the morning she did not feel better. Nor the next day nor the day after that. Then one day as the sun lit up the sea with silver she awoke to see a thin line of green on the horizon. Paulus came to the opening of her little cubby hole and looking at her dishevelled state he smiled.

"See that land over there?"

"Yes."

"That's Britannia."

Suddenly the discomfort of the previous days disappeared and Cornelia went to stand at the rail and gazed towards the horizon. Then turning to Paulus she said "I'm hungry."

"I'm not surprised, Hector's had more to eat than you have over the last few days."

The cook, seeing Cornelia standing at the rail came over with a steaming bowl of gruel.

"Here you are. This will put the colour back in your cheeks."

Never had gruel tasted so good. It was well sweetened with honey and had the desired effect.

Early next morning the ship was rowed into harbour and Paulus and Cornelia took their leave of the Captain and crew.

"If ever you want to go to sea again I'd be happy to take you on," the Captain said to Paulus. "You're a hard worker with good sea-legs."

"I thank you sir, but I feel I won't be leaving home again for some time."

They turned their backs on the sea and walked into the town. At the edge of town they came to a main road that led in a west/east direction.

"Which way should we go?" said Cornelia.

Coming towards them was a cart being pulled slowly by a

single ox driven by a man in a country style tunic.

The cart contained two squealing pigs. Paulus hailed the driver.

"Which road is this?" he asked. "Where does it lead?"

"Well, if you go east you'll get to Noviomagus then north to Londinium. But you can go more east but I don't know where that leads, I've never been beyond the crossroads."

"My thanks to you. I hope you get a good price for your swine."

The farmer touched his ox with his stick and grunted at it to pull away. As he disappeared down the road Paulus said "We should go east then ask again in the next town."

Noviomagus was closer than they thought and there they decided to take the road north. Paulus reasoned that when they went to Londinium on their visit the road was no more than half a day's journey from their home so they should eventually come upon some familiar landmark or hill. In Noviomagus they stocked up on provisions for the journey but decided not to stop at midday. They walked along munching apples and taking it in turns to tear lumps from a loaf with their teeth. The sun was going down when tiredness and hunger forced them to a stop. Cornelia set about gathering sticks for a fire but as she climbed to the top of a small hill at the road-side she spied a light in the distance.

"Paulus," she called.

As he came up to her she pointed to the light.

"That looks like a farmhouse or perhaps a villa," she said.

"It's only about half a mile off, lets walk there."

As they approached they saw that indeed is was a small farm and they were able to purchase a hot if simple meal and the farmer said they were welcome to sleep in the barn. Next morning they broke their fast on gruel and giving the farmer some coins for his hospitality they set on their way.

Next day around midday they found themselves gazing over miles of undulating farmland with woods here and there.

"I recognise that skyline," said Paulus. "I'm sure that's the skyline that we see from the hill with the fallen stone near home."

Cornelia agreed and they set off again with renewed vigour. The afternoon was declining when they came upon the road which they both knew led to home. They had gone down the road no more that a mile and a half when suddenly Hector lifted his head and sniffed the air. Then giving a little yelp of pleasure he set off at a determined trot.

In spite of their tiredness a new spring came into their steps and as they rounded the next bend there ahead of them was their home. As they drew near Cornelia suddenly started to feel apprehensive.

"Do you think they'll be pleased to see us or do you think they'll be cross?" she said.

"I'm sure they'll be pleased to see us and I think they will probably be too surprised to be cross," Paulus replied.

They decided to go to the main door rather than enter through the yard at the side. Paulus raised his fist and knocked on the door. They heard steps on the other side and Hector gave out a little whine and wagged his tail. The door was opened by Florens who stood there and stared open-mouthed at them.

"Who is it?" came a voice that Cornelia recognised as her mother's.

"It's me Mother," she said as she stepped over the threshold. Her mother came hurrying into the entrance hall and after a few seconds during which she stood and stared at the home comers with a look of disbelief she rushed to her daughter and threw her arms around her. They stood hugging each other and alternately crying and laughing while Paulus stood and waited.

Suddenly Cornelia's father came to see what all the commotion was about and he too stopped short at the sight of his daughter. He stood stunned for a long moment, then snatched her from her mother's arms and hugged her to him.

"Where in Hades have you been, you naughty girl?"

Then he turned his attention to Paulus.

"I said I'd bring her back, Master. I'm sorry it took so long." Gaius gave him a warm pat on the shoulder.

"I'm sure there is a great deal to tell but now go and see your father and come and see me after dinner."

Verina ordered Florens to take hot water to Cornelia's room and help her to prepare herself for dinner. Hector, once the greetings and fuss were over trotted off in the direction of the kitchen as Cornelia went to wash off the dust of the road and change for dinner.

She was sitting in the triclinium with her parents waiting for the food to be served. A slave poured goblets of wine and water and she looked at her parents. They both looked older, much older than she would have thought they would be after less than two years. Her mother's face was lined and her expression sad, even though she was glad of the return of her daughter. Her father's hair had become sparser and what he had had turned grey. He seemed to be worrying about something.

"Where's Jo?" asked Cornelia. "Will he be joining us?"

Both her parents looked at her and then at each other as if they were not sure what to answer. Then her father looked into her face and said

"Your brother is dead."

Cornelia gasped and stared at her parents then huge tears started to roll down her cheeks.

"When, how did it happen?" she asked between sobs.

"About a year ago," said her father. "One of the men was cleaning out the piggery and Jo went to oversee the work. He slipped in the mud and grazed his leg. It didn't seem like a bad wound at the time but next day it was red and painful and in spite of your mother's care it would not heal. The poison went into his blood and he grew weaker and weaker and more and more fevered and a week later he died."

Cornelia did not know what to say. Her heart felt like a stone in her chest .

"Drink some wine. After dinner I will show you his grave and you can say your goodbyes and perhaps make a prayer."

The food was served and they ate in silence. Cornelia could not say what she had eaten and found it hard to look at her parents. She felt guilty about having been away during Jo's death. After dinner Verina and Cornelia donned their capes and went out to see Jo's grave. Gaius went to his study and was sitting staring into space when a slave showed Paulus in.

"I'm sorry we were away so long," Paulus said "but your daughter refused to come home. I promised you I would see that she came to no harm so I felt I had no choice but to accompany her. She is a very strong minded young lady."

"You could say that," said Gaius. "I"d be more inclined to call her obstinate. However, I'm very grateful to you for protecting her and bringing her back safely. We have missed her a great deal; and I know your father missed you. We won't go into all the details of your excursion tonight, there'll be time enough for that. Now we have to make some decisions about the farm and the work you will be required to take on now that Jo is gone."

"Master, can I say how sad I am to hear of his death, he was a friend to me and I respected him."

"Thank you."

"However, I have something very important I wish to say to you."

Gaius looked up at Paulus inquiringly. Paulus unhooked a leather pouch from his belt and placed in on the table. As Gaius picked it up it chinked. He untied the thong at the neck and tipped a heap of gold coins onto the table. He looked at it in amazement.

"What is this? Where did it come from?"

"It was a gift from a wealthy Roman for saving his son in an accident. I want to buy my freedom and that of my father."

Gaius stared at the coins for a long, silent moment. Then he looked up. "Take a chair and sit down," he told Paulus. "We have a lot to talk about."

Paulus drew a chair up to the desk and sat facing Gaius.

"Since you went away and Jo died things have been very difficult here. Last season the harvest was bad, but things were made worse by the departure of the cavalry that were stationed over at Onna as apart from having a poor harvest we lost a big customer. When Jo died I could not see the point in struggling on with the farm. After all, who was it for? Crassus came to me only a week ago and offered to buy most of my land. It adjoins his and he wants to increase his holding. We would keep our villa and the orchard and the money he would pay us would make it possible for my wife and I to end our days here in comfort. What do you think I should do?"

Paulus looked at Gaius intently. It was not normal for a Master to ask a mere slave for his opinion on such an important issue.

"Could you not use this money to tide us over the winter and buy seed for next year's crops? The army will not leave a place like Onna empty for long, and by next year we should be secure once more."

Gaius smiled. "Does that mean that you intend to stay? With your freedom would you and your father not wish to leave and make your own way in the world?"

"Master I, that is we, would never leave. This is our home. To see Rome was a wonderful experience but I never stopped hoping we would eventually return."

"Then will you stay and help me work the farm? Of course you would both be paid a remuneration."

"Of course we'll stay."

Gaius breathed a sigh of relief and looked more peaceful than he had for months.

"If things were going well and you had asked me to grant your freedom I would have given it to you for nothing in recognition of your service. However, as we are on hard times I shall use your gold but in return I will appoint you as my estate manager . Are you in accordance and prepared to shoulder the responsibility?"

"Sir, there is one other thing."

"Name it".

"As I am now a freedman I would like your permission to ask your daughter to become my wife."

If Gaius was surprised before, now he was amazed.

"What does Cornelia say?" he asked.

"She doesn't know. I wanted to have your permission first but if she is against it rest assured no-one will hear any more of it, even if she decides to marry Crassus."

Gaius gave a sudden grin. "Thankfully she can't do that, Crassus got married last summer to that little mouse of a girl whose father owns the big grain store over at Venta Belgarum. It seems that once he could not get his hands on our land by marriage, a grain export business seemed a good prospect. She is soon to present him with their first child. He and Cornelia would never have got on together, she's far too headstrong , they would have fought tooth and nail."

Paulus smiled.

"I will let you know what Cornelia's reply is," said Paulus.

"Thank you," said Gaius warmly, "and thank you for bringing our daughter home safely."

"It was the least I could do, but I have to admit it wasn't always easy."

As Paulus rose to leave the room both men were smiling.

Cornelia and her mother walked through the orchard and went out through a side gate into the field above the meadow. There in a corner of the field facing down the slope to the brook stood a fresh, white gravestone. It was simply engraved "Here lies Jovianus son of Gaius. Died in his 22nd year."

Cornelia stood silently looking at it for a while then wept afresh. She said to her mother

"I did love him. I know wc quarrelled and I would not obey him, but I did love him."

"I know you did, and he was sorry he could not say his goodbyes to you."

The two women stood with their arms about each other's waist.

"I'm sorry I gave you so much pain," said Cornelia, "but I really did love Marcus. We were betrothed in Rome. He came from a very good family and they all treated me very kindly, but Marcus was killed in a battle. He never knew I was expecting his baby but when he died I lost the baby. I'm so sorry for what I did."

"I expect you couldn't help yourself. Never mind, it's all over now and we must look ahead."

"If you want me to I'll marry Crassus."

"Do you like Crassus?" asked Verina, surprised.

"No, but I've caused you enough sorrow."

"Well I'm glad to say you can't marry Crassus, he's already married."

"Oh, thank goodness for that" said Cornelia, and they both laughed.

As they opened the gate and went back into the orchard a figure detached itself from the shadows and came forward as if it had been waiting for them. It was Paulus who, after greeting Verina politely asked Cornelia if she would like to come and see the foal that had been born just before her departure. Verina turned towards the house and Cornelia and Paulus made their way across the orchard. As they approached the meadow Cornelia said "Why are we going down here? Isn't the horse in the stable?"

"You can see the horse tomorrow, I have something to tell you."

They walked together in the gathering dusk down to the river bank and sat on a fallen tree trunk.

"Remember when we used to bathe here as children," said Cornelia.

"Yes, and how we used to catch minnows."

"We really had a very happy childhood. Now that you're grown up do you mind being a slave?"

"That's what I wanted to talk to you about. I'm not a slave

any longer. I have bought my freedom."

"Oh," was all Cornelia could think to say. Then after a moment's thought she added, "Does that mean you are going to go away?" Suddenly home without Paulus seemed a very sad place.

"No, I'm not going away. Your father asked me to stay on here as estate manager. That's another thing I wanted to talk to you about. Will you consent to be my wife?"

She looked at him in amazement than as she realised the full implication of what he had said her face softened and broke into a smile.

"Of course, if you feel you need time to think about it to get used to the idea there's no rush. I've waited most of my life for you, a little longer won't matter."

"I don't need time to think about it. I can't imagine life without you. Of course I'll marry you," and he took her gently in his arms and they kissed deeply and fondly.

As they drew apart Paulus said "I have something for you."

He put his hand in the pocket of his tunic and pulled out a bracelet. It was made from a boar's tooth which had been highly polished and capped at the base with finely wrought gold. As he slipped it onto her arm she said,

"Paulus, it's beautiful. Where did you buy it?"

"I didn't buy it. Don't you remember? It's from the boar I killed when we left. The goldsmith in Rome took the other one as payment for doing the work."

"Paulus, it's the most beautiful thing I've ever had." and she embraced him warmly.

About Bretwalda Books

Bretwalda Books is an exciting new publishing company devoted to exploring the lesser known areas of British and European history. We aim to produce books targetted at the general market embracing popular writing styles and attractive design formats while upholding the highest standards of accuracy and reliability. Our books will deal with unusual topics in an open and engaging manner.

All our books are available as ebooks on Kindle, Kobo, Apple and other major ebook shops.

Why Bretwalda?

The term "Bretwalda" is one of the more mysterious titles in Dark Age British History. It has been translated in various ways and although entire nations were plunged into war and thousands of men were killed fighting for the right to use the title, nobody is entirely certain what it meant. We thought it summed up our mission to uncover the little known nooks and crannies of history. In fact, that gives us an idea for a book ...

Finding Bretwalda

Bretwalda has a constantly growing range of innovative books.

We have a website on
www.BretwaldaBooks.com

We have a blog on
http://bretwaldabooks.blogspot.com/

We have a Facebook Page as
Bretwalda Books

We have a Twitter account as
@Bretwaldabooks

You can email us on
info@bretwaldabooks.com

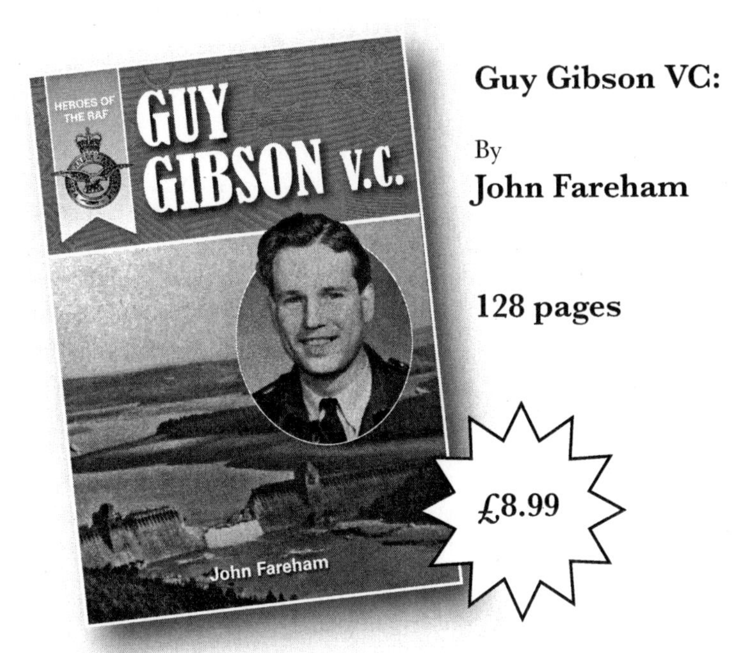

Guy Gibson VC:

By
John Fareham

128 pages

Thrilling biography of the man who led the Dambusters Raid. Having joined the RAF in 1936, Gibson was a bomber pilot when war broke out. He won a DFC in July 1940 then volunteered for Fighter Command and flew nightfighters on 99 sorites before returning to Bomber Command to fly 46 more missions before the Dambusters Raid. This book looks at the life and career of the man who led the most famous bombing raid of World War II. It is a gripping account of his life and exploits, revealing new and little known facts about Guy Gibson for the first time.

About the Author

JOHN FAREHAM is the son of an RAF veteran who grew up on RAF bases around the world. He now lives only a short drive from RAF Scampton from which Gibson flew his famous Dambuster Raid.

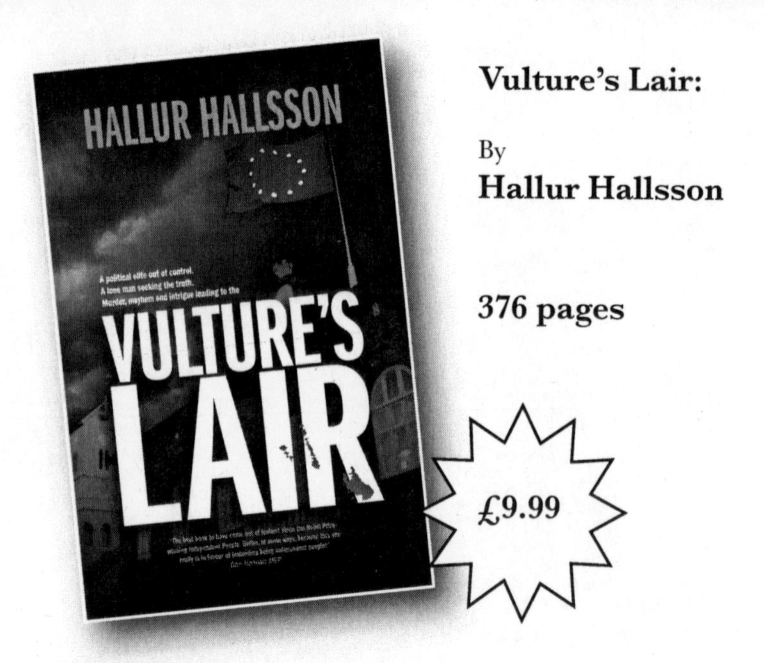

Vulture's Lair:

By
Hallur Hallsson

376 pages

£9.99

The first great eurosceptic novel that the world has been waiting for.

BRUSSELS. Krummi the fisherman leads a protest against corrupt EU regulations and uncovers a desperate secret.

BERLIN. A sinister figure in a black suit deep inside the hierarchy plots a coup with politics, big business and the Mafia to plunge Europe into dictatorship.

Can Krummi stay alive long to find out what is really happening? Can he stop the Vulture? And will he ever discover where to find the Vulture's Lair?

About the Author

HALLUR HALLSSON is a leading journalist and TV-personality in Iceland. Hallsson was one of the founders of the daily Dagbladid in 1975 which became the second biggest newspaper in Iceland. He was a leading journalist at the influential Morgunbladid and a journalist and anchor at Channel 2 and State Television.

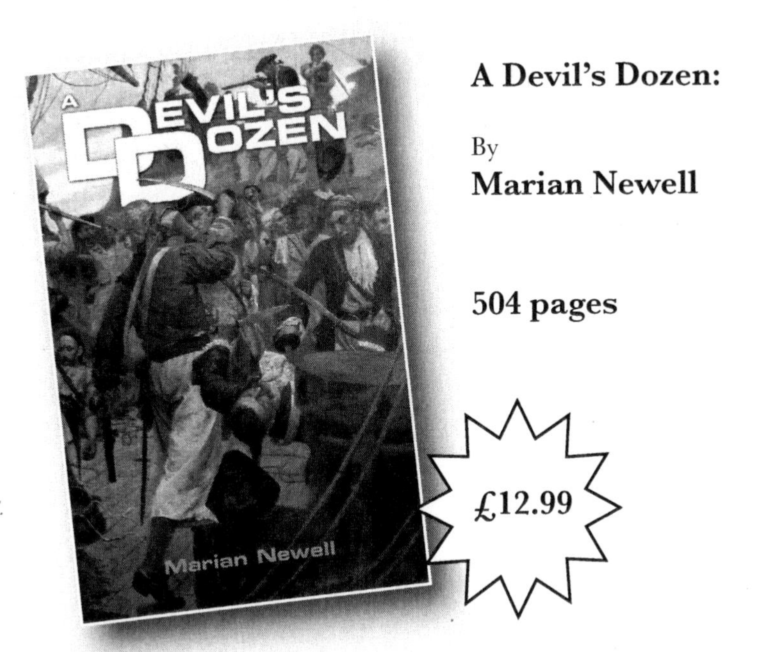

A Devil's Dozen:

By
Marian Newell

504 pages

Violence, love, loyalty and betrayal among the smugglers who terrorise the coasts of southern England. For years the Aldington Blues and the Burmarsh Gang have fought each other over the lucrative smuggling trade in Kent. But the spectre of the gallows hangs over them all when a popular naval officer is killed by a smuggler. As the government men close in, the gangs join forces. But will it be enough to stave off defeat, capture and death? Meticulously researched, "A Devil's Dozen" recreates the vanished world of the smugglers who were once the kings of the British underworld.

About the Author

MARIAN NEWELL has lived all her life in the land where the smugglers once held sway. She grew up hearing the tales of those days and now has written them up in fictionalised form as her first published book.

Bretwalda Books Ltd

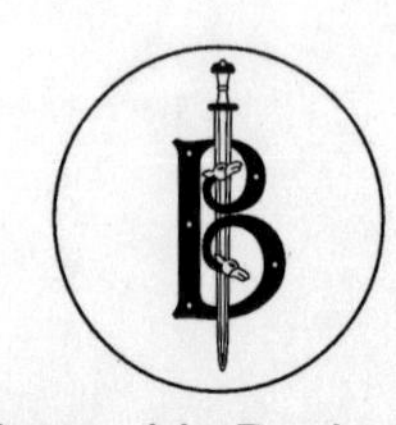

Bretwalda Books Ltd